3

talking to the enemy
stories

avner mandelman

SEVEN STORIES PRESS

New York•London•Toronto•Melbourne

Seven Stories Press
140 Watts Street
New York, NY 10013
www.sevenstories.com

In the U.K.:
Turnaround Publisher Services Ltd., Unit 3, Olympia Trading Estate, Coburg Road, Wood Green, London N22 6TZ

In Australia:
Palgrave Macmillan, 627 Chapel Street, South Yarra VIC 3141

Library of Congress Cataloging-in-Publication Data
Mandelman, Avner.
  Talking to the enemy : stories / Avner Mandelman.—A Seven Stories Press 1st ed.
      p. cm.
  ISBN 1-58322-669-9 (hardcover : alk. paper)
  1. Israel—Social life and customs—Fiction. 2. Jews—Israel—Fiction. I. Title.
PR9199.3.M34814T35 2005
813'.54—dc22   2004023304

9 8 7 6 5 4 3 2 1

College professors may order examination copies of Seven Stories Press titles for a free six-month trial period. To order, visit www.sevenstories.com/textbook, or fax on school letterhead to (212) 226-1411.

Book design by Jon Gilbert
Printed in Canada

Contents

Pity

We've been watching him for two weeks, Léon and I, from inside a shop across the avenue Foch. It belonged to a local Jew who helped the Mossad every now and then, and didn't ask any questions. This time he closed his shop for us—I didn't ask how much it was costing him. It was a posh boutique, with chinchilla and astrakhan coats hanging under Tiffany lamps and mink jackets in the corners, and Léon and I made ourselves at home, taking turns at the Zeiss monoscope behind the curtain. We watched the second-floor apartment across the avenue, where the man who called himself Charles LeGrand now lived.

Until the month before we weren't even sure it was he; but then the local Mossad *katsa* broke into the office of LeGrand's dentist in Neuilly, made copies of his x-rays and sent them to the archive of *Yad VaShem*, and after a week the answer came back that it was indeed he, Karl Joachim Gross, The Smiler himself. In '43, he had personally supervised the killing of five, maybe six thousand Jews in the Lodz ghetto, two thousand of them children, and who knows how many more in Maidanek. Not a very big fish, compared to Eichmann and Mengele, but a fish just the same. Took us five years to locate him, once it was decided to go one level down, since we had gotten all the ones above him already. The funny thing is, the HQ for catching Nazi fugitives was in Paris, and Gross was number three on our list, yet it took us that long to find him. We had looked for him in Rio, and La Paz, even in Santiago, and here he was all the time in avenue Foch, right between our legs, 400 metres away from our own consul's apartment.

This Gross, he now owned a little newspaper by the name of *Vents Neufs*, New Winds, a liberal paper, supportive of Israel, culture, art, shit like that. Most probably as camouflage, because fuckers like him never change. It's in the blood, whatever it is. He was old now, more than 70, though he carried himself as erect as if he were De Gaulle, or something, and he lived on the second floor of a grey apartment building on the good side of the avenue, the north side, with two poodles, a little girl (his grand-daughter, maybe, or a niece), and a blond Swedish nurse or a nanny, whatever she was, that took care of the girl, maybe of him, too. We didn't care about her, or the girl. Only him. I especially. My grandparents went in the Lodz ghetto, also two uncles, three aunts, and all my cousins. Only my father escaped.

At first, after I had tracked Gross down in Paris, the *Memuneh*, the Mossad's chief, got cold feet and wanted to take me off the case. But then my father intervened and said I was a pro, he had trained me himself, I could handle it, they shouldn't insult me, this and that. So they let me continue, but they glued Léon Aboulafia to me, a Moroccan Jew from Casablanca, who knew Nazis only from the movies, from Tach'kemoni high school, and maybe also from *Yad VaShem*, but that's it. Eichmann, too, they had let only

Moroccan Jews guard him. I mean, we are all good soldiers and obey orders, but why take chances.

So we had been watching this Gross for two weeks, pigging out on *boeuf en croûte* and croissants and fancy cheeses that the local Shadowers who kept a back-up team in a café nearby left us every morning at the back door, when we finally got the go-ahead, straight from the *Midrasha* in Tel Aviv. The embassy *bodel*, a short fat woman by the name of Varda, came by one evening and slid an envelope into the mail-slot in the front door, just like that, with the code word *Sun in Giv'on*, which meant we could take him, and it was up to us how to do it.

The orders, when we had left Tel Aviv, were to take Gross alive, bring him to Yerushalayim for a trial, but if anything went wrong, not to think twice, to take him down immediately, silent or noisy, then scram to London via Calais, where two DST border guards were on our payroll.

It went without saying that taking down Gross would look bad for me, what with my father's intervention, and the *Memuneh* breaking the rules for me, and everything. "But better this than headlines," my father said, when right after Léon and I had landed in Paris, I called him from a hookers' café in Pigalle, going through one of our Zurich lines. "If you got to take him down, do it."

"No, I'll bring him alive, don't worry," I said.

"But don't take chances. I don't want to see you with *tzitzes* on your back." Which meant, "I don't want to see you on the front cover of *Ha'Olam HaZeh.*"

Ha'Olam HaZeh is the yellow rag of Israel. The back pages show women with exposed *tzitzes* , the front cover exposes the political scandal of the day.

"Oh, don't worry," I said. "I'll bring him. Nobody'll know anything, until he's in the glass booth."

The glass booth was where Eichmann had sat for his trial, so a crazed survivor of some camp couldn't shoot him or something.

There was a little pause. All around me were hookers, cackling in argot.

"Don't worry," I said again. "He'll be there soon."

"With God's help," my father said. (He had become religious in his old age, after he had retired.) "With God's help."

"With, without, you get the cage ready," I said, "he'll be there."

This was two weeks before. Now it was Friday night. I had been watching the literary program "Apostrophes" on the small television, using the earphones, and Léon was at the 'scope, when the envelope slid in. We both knew what it was, even before Léon clicked open his *katsa* knife and slit it open.

It took him two minutes to decipher the message with his *Tzadi-Aleph*.

"Mother's cunt," Léon said to me in Hebrew, after finishing the computation. "We go."

Usually we spoke French, in case someone heard voices inside. But I guess he got excited. Take-downs he had done already, two, maybe three, but this was his first abduction, and a Nazi, too.

I myself had done three abductions before, two of them in Europe, one in Cairo. None was a Nazi, but so what. Nazis, Arabs, they are all the same to me. Haters of Yisrael, destroyers of Ya'acov, as the Bible said, it is a *mitzvah* to persecute them, to exterminate them to the tenth generation, like King Shaul was supposed to do to the Amalekite, by the order of God, when he foolishly took pity on his enemy and so lost his kingship. We learned about this, in the *Midrasha*, in the *katsa* course; about the dangers of having a soft heart. No pity or compassion for these fuckers. None.

Not that I had any fear, now, of this. If anything, it was just the opposite. I knew the stories as well as anyone, what the old hands said, that there was nothing like catching a Nazi—it's better than sex, getting your hands on one of them, a real live one, being part of God's own Sword of Vengeance, so to speak. Even experienced *katsas* sometimes went crazy, when they saw a Nazi up close. Six years ago in Buenos Aires, two *katsas* from *Eytanim* department, the Russian shadowers, with fifteen years service between them, slit the throat of an old hag they were supposed to bring in, some Austrian nurse who was said to have helped Mengele do selections. Her trial in Yerushalayim was ready to begin, with documents stacked a metre high, Golda's speech to the Knesset already printed in large type, so she could read it to the TV cameras without glasses, the editors' committee already briefed, everything, when suddenly, the night before shipment, the Nazi hag said a few words to one of them, maybe spit in his face, something, and they slit her throat. Just like that, both of them, one after the other. They were not even Ashkenazi Jews, or anything. One a Moroccan, like Léon, the other a Jerusalemite, his parents originally from Turkey, both sets of grandparents still living, even; still they did her, not a second thought. Go learn why. Maybe it's in the genes, now, this hatred. Like men and snakes, forever and ever, with no forgiveness possible.

Later the two were demoted of course, but after less than six months they both got their ranks back, after Golda personally intervened on their behalf with my father, who was the *Memuneh* then. Because who can say he would have behaved differently? she said. Who can say he would have stayed his hand? Orders are orders, but sometimes there's a limit.

A week in that furrier boutique, still waiting for the go-ahead, that's exactly what I had begun to feel. Ten days, and still nothing. By then I was really beginning to worry, because you never know, someone might have gotten it into his head to cancel. Who knows what goes on in the corridors in the *Q'irya*, in Tel Aviv, or in the Knesset committees, in Yerushalayim, with all these soft-hearted kibbutzniks. I even suggested to Léon, once, to do it before any orders arrived, then tell the *Midrasha* we were faced with f.c.r.i., field-circumstances-requiring-initiative. But Léon said no. It was too this, it was too that, and I didn't argue with him too much, because, let's face it, I didn't want to make more of a mess than we had to, and also because of my father, and the *Memuneh*, and everything. But with every day that passed, my obedience was weakening, because I was getting sicker and sicker of seeing this Gross strolling down the avenue with the poodle leash in one hand, the little girl's hand in the other, the nurse behind. Every time I saw him ambling by, happy and smiling and pink, not more than five metres away, I had to stop myself from rushing out to stick a tape over his white smile, throw him in the vw van, then drive the parcel to the Israeli embassy and let the resident *katsa* take care of the rest. I mean, the consul would have *plotzed*, since it would have made him directly involved. But what the hell, we could, if we had to. In such matters we outranked him and he knew it.

Anyway, the orders came, so the only thing left to do, beside the actual job, was decide when and how to do it, and how to ship him over. Finally (it took three hours of arguing), we decided to bag Gross on Sunday. (Sunday mornings he went with his little grand-daughter, or niece, or whatever she was, to La Madeleine church, without the nurse.) We would then ship him out to Israel the very same night, no delay.

Now, normally, shipping him would have been an Aleph-Aleph

problem, because after Switzerland, which is a complete police state, where the SSHD always knows when every foreigner farts, France is the worst place in Europe. In Switzerland they are at least polite to you, and also are honest and stay bribed, once you pay them off. But these French fuckers—everybody, flics, DST, SDECE, CRS—they'll all happily take whatever you slip them, stick it in their ass-pocket, then go and haul you in anyway and divide the loot with the boss. That's the national character. Whores from birth, is what they are. No wonder they all collaborated with the Nazis in the forties, helped them ship the Jews to the camps, also managed some of the local camps for them, from Vichy. Fucking bastards, the Nazis and the French both. I once saw the train station on the outskirts of Paris, near the Port de Clignancourt, from where they had sent the Jews east—a crumbling structure and rusty rails, not even a sign of what had once happened there. Not a plaque, not a note, nothing. Sometimes I wish I had been born then, so I could fight the fuckers when they were still young, like my father did, after he got out of the Polish forests and roamed all over Europe with a pair of knives and a Luger, and a little notebook where he kept score in *Rashi* Hebrew script. But we can't all be lucky.

This time, though, it seemed we were: two of our missile boats were docked in Marseille, for installation of these new CW radars from Dassault, and Thomson CSF digital sonar, that the local *katsa* had bribed out of the Defence Ministry, and by chance I knew the captain of one of them—also a Tel Avivi boy, by the name of Amirav Feiglin, who had once been with me in Young Maccabi, and also later, in Flight Course, which we both flunked. Years before, in Wormaiza Street, he had once stolen my bike, and when I caught him I of course beat him up, but I also let him beat me back a little, and we remained friends. So now, when Saturday morning

Varda arrived for last-minute instructions, I asked her to send Ami a message in *Tzadi-Tzadi*, regular IDF MilCode, bypassing the embassy *katsa*, and ask him if he would take a live package with him on the boat to Haifa, in a large box, and also us, Léon and me, without passports.

Varda made a face when I asked her to bypass the embassy *katsa*, but she agreed, as I knew she would. I used to fuck her, two years before, when she was new in the Paris station and not yet so fat from all this Parisian butter. I was stationed in Paris then for a series of take-downs of some local PLO *shawishes*, who had helped blow up two El Al offices, and she was the decoy, masquerading as a hooker. Old business, this, doesn't matter. The main thing is, she agreed to give Ami the message, and also help drive the van.

"You need anything else?" she asked, after I had finished telling her what I wanted.

She had entered the boutique via the side door, and now sat in the purple armchair of the furrier's customers, rubbing her cheek on a white astrakhan coat that cost maybe 200,000 francs, maybe more. Her freckled face, under the thick makeup, was still pretty, also her tits were still upright; only her flanks had begun to go flabby and her ankles had thickened, maybe from all this walking, trailing people, eating on the run. Also, two years ago, she was told to put on weight, because Arabs like them fat, and now it was probably hard to take it off. It's not the healthiest thing, being a junior embassy *katsa*. But what do you want, there are worse things than giving your youth to your people. At least there's still a people to give it to.

"Yes," said Léon, "syringes, tapes, sack, everything."

He, too, had fucked her once or twice, I am sure, for form's sake, when he had arrived in Paris. But of course it was no big deal. In the Mossad, fucking is like a handshake. It's a greeting to a colleague. It's even sort of encouraged, so you don't have people falling in love with each other, or something, screwing up the operational chain of command. If everyone screws everyone, it doesn't matter anymore, and you can direct your mind to more important stuff. Anyway, that's the theory. I remember how after fucking Varda exclusively for more than a year, I was told several times to look around, there were more women in the Mossad, a new crop every year coming from the *Midrasha*, what did I get stuck on this fat broad for. (She wasn't that fat, then.) Finally, I got the hint and stopped it; or maybe she did, I can't remember. Maybe she got the hint, too. This was just after the business with the PLO *shawishes*. Anyway, it was a long while back.

She said now, "Maybe you need more people?"

I saw she was eager to get in on the thing, not just to drive. Catching a live Nazi, it doesn't come up every day.

"No," I said. "Léon and I are enough, for this."

"Sure," Léon said. "It's a small job."

His first abduction, already an expert.

"No, I can help, too," Varda said. "Really."

I saw she didn't get it, so I said, "You are also a Polack, a Bilavsky, they won't let you."

Couldn't she see it? The orders were to bring him alive, that's why there were only two of us, in a job that required four at least. To minimize the chances of a repeat of the Buenos Aires fuck-up.

"Only on my father's side," Varda said. "My mother was from Greece."

"Same thing."

The Nazis had also killed half the Jews of Greece, and sent the other half to Auschwitz. I was once in Salonika with a small back-up team from *Kardomm*, on a take-down job of a PLO mechanic. On my day off I went to the local Jewish cemetery. It was so full of headstones, you could hardly walk. If Tito hadn't stopped them in Yugoslavia, and Montgomery in El Alamein, these fuckers would have done the same in Tel Aviv, brought down the Third Temple. Touch and go, it was. Touch and go.

Varda said, "No, I got my Authorization last month. Really."

"Congratulations," Léon drawled. "Commander."

The Authorization is a permission to kill without having your life or the life of a colleague threatened, based on f.c.r.i. It's roughly equivalent to an officer's commission in the Army.

Varda's nose turned red. "No, really. So if you need someone."

I began to say it was okay by me, but Léon said quickly it was not something he wanted to take on. Maybe because she was half a Polack, or maybe because he did not want a woman on the job. Moroccans are like that. Women for them are good only for one thing, babies. Maybe for fucking, too, but even for this they prefer each other.

"Authorization, shmauthorization," Léon said. "You want to help drive, fine, drive, but this thing, Mickey and I do it."

He said it as if he was giving the orders all of a sudden, and I got mad. I said if she wanted to help, let her help, why not? Maybe we could use a woman.

"Like how, use?" Léon said. "We don't need anybody else. Two is enough, for this, mother's cunt, an old man and a little girl!"

I said, "But if, I don't know, the little girl shouts, or something."

"So what? Mother's cunt! She shouts, he shouts, anyone shouts, it's the same thing. Anything goes wrong, we take him down, ten seconds, we are gone."

"You or me?" I said. "Who will do him? If we have to."

Léon got all red in the neck. He knew very well that the one who took down Gross would have it on his file forever. The Panicker, the one who had screwed up The Smiler's trial. But if he now said I should do it, if we had to, it would be like admitting he didn't have the stomach for it.

Varda looked at me with professional admiration, at how I had hemmed Léon in. But I didn't give a shit about that, now. "So who would do him?" I asked again.

"We won't have to," Léon said at last, his voice sandy.

"And if he fights?"

I don't know why I was so mad at Léon, all of a sudden.

"So he fights!" Léon snarled. "So he fights! Lift some weights tonight, so you can bend his arm!"

Varda said pacifically, "This Swedish nurse, she could make trouble, if she comes, or the girl, what do I know."

Léon snapped at her that he would ask for her opinion if he wanted it.

"Fuck you," Varda snapped back at him. "Fuck you, ya Aboulafia, you speak nicely or I'll take off your left ball."

I liked her again, now. That's the way.

"It's too big for you," Léon said.

"An olive, I bet," Varda said, which was nice of her, too, implying she had never seen it.

There was a short silence while we regrouped, so to speak, picking at the cheese, pouring chambertin, passing napkins.

Finally, Léon said the nurse never came on Sundays. The shadowers had told us so.

I said nothing. Both he and I knew that this did not mean a thing. The shadowers fucked up half the time. A bunch of Yemenite boys good for nothing. Only because of the coalition agreement did they take them in at all.

"Yeah," I said at last, not wishing to restart anything. It would all go on our report anyway, every word of this, from the tape recorder, which we had to leave open by standing orders.

"But I can take care of her," Varda said, not making clear whether she had meant the nurse, if she came, or the girl.

"No, no," Léon said. "Mickey and I will do it. It'll be a breeze."

"So anyway, if you need me."

"Fine, fine," Léon snapped. "We heard you."

But of course it wasn't a breeze.

I had the first inkling of this the next morning, when we parked the vw van on rue Blé, a quiet side-street forking off the north end of avenue Foch, waiting for Gross to appear.

Half an hour and he hadn't come yet.

"Abort," I said to Léon. "He's late. Late! Something is wrong. Abort, Léon, abort!"

Taking down Gross, each one of us could decide on his own, and justify later. But aborting on lateness, for this we needed a consensus.

"Nah," Léon said. "Don't be a *yachne*. He had a diarrhea, from too much cheese, or maybe a hangover. Something."

Fifteen minutes more. Still nothing.

"Abort!" I said.

"You want to veto?" Léon said. "On your head."

I thought about it. Aborting on a hunch was permissible, but if it came out later it was nothing, I would be a *yachne* forever. An old woman. Not in my file, but where it counts. In the *Midrasha*'s cafeteria, in the *Sayeret*'s summer camp, in the hotel safe rooms.

"It's a Nazi," Varda said. Her face had become puffy, as if air was blowing through it, from within. "A fucking Nazi. You won't wait for him a half-hour?"

"All right," I said at last. "For a Nazi I'll wait."

Ten minutes more. Fifty minutes late.

"Relax," Léon said to me. "It's still quiet."

Indeed, rue Blé was deserted. Even avenue Foch had almost no cars. Maybe a cab or two going to Neuilly.

"Yeah," I said, grudgingly. "It's quiet."

Maybe it would still be all right.

But when Gross finally came around the corner, embalmed in a black suit and sporting a dark Tyrolean hat, it was plain for all to see that it was an Aleph-Aleph fuck-up.

He was holding the girl in one hand, the Swedish nurse in the other, and behind the nurse, all holding hands, were a bunch of little girls all dressed in black, squeaking and chirping like blackbirds. (Later we learned it was the niece's birthday, and her lycée friends had all come along, for church.)

"Shit in yoghurt!" Varda said in Hebrew.

I said nothing, but it was obviously a disaster.

Without looking at me, Léon said we should abort. "Just let him go, we'll come back next week."

But now I, all of a sudden, was hot to trot. Maybe because, I don't know, I saw him now before me. The bright smile, the upturned old nose, the soft white hands.

"No," I said to Léon. "Let's get him."

Léon, crouching near his own eyehole, at the van's door, shook his head, so I grabbed his shoulders and said the missile boats were leaving Marseille the next day. If we postponed, we'd have to wait another week, dump Gross in the embassy, to be sent on El Al as diplomatic cargo, in a box, then he might die en route, there'd be no trial, nothing, only bureaucratic shit forever and ever. "You want Bleiman telexing Glilot for the next hundred years?"

Yoram Bleiman was our consul in Paris—his daughter was married to the PM's younger son, the one who avoided military service by going to a Yeshiva. I knew for a fact the PM could stand neither one of the three; but did I want my fuck-ups coming up at Friday eve meals at the PM's table for the next five years? Also, I could see my own father giving me that pained look, across our own Friday table. (After my mother died I went to live with him, in our old apartment, on Wormaiza Street.)

"So he'll telex," Léon said. "Let him telex."

"All right, sure," I said. "Let's go back, have one more croissant, wait another week, maybe they'll send another team, an experienced one. Maybe a bunch of Yemenites they'd pull off some tail-job, in Cyprus."

Léon got all white around the nose. For a brief moment I thought he would punch me. Then he got up from the floor. "All right, fuck it, let's go."

Even this late on a Sunday morning, perhaps ten o'clock already, rue Blé was still deserted as a lane in Yerushalayim on Yom Kippur. The café-tabacs were all shuttered, the lottery office closed, not even pigeons on the sidewalks. Aside from the squealing little girls, it was calm and quiet. We might even have had the required 30 seconds to do it—rush out when he was passing the pâtisserie, grab him, inject him, and throw him in, all in one movement (a dozen times we had practiced this, before we left Tel Aviv), but because we had hesitated and argued, Gross had already passed us by. So when we finally jumped out, clanging the van's door open in our haste, he turned, and stared at us. His cheeks got all tight and military—he knew on the instant—and then his face fell apart and he screamed. It was a scream the likes of which I had never heard before, worse than if someone had slit his throat open.

And then everything got fucked up all to hell.

The Swedish nurse, as if she had practiced this before, bashed Léon on the back of the head with both fists, twice, and he fell as if he was made of wood, straight forward, mashing his nose on the pavement: there was a loud crack, like a piece of lumber breaking, and blood squirted out of his face as if a faucet had burst.

All the little girls began to scream, the whole lot of them, and scurry about like crazed mice, and by that time Gross was running down rue Blé—72 years old, but loping ahead like a deer toward avenue Foch. Then the Swedish nurse threw herself on me, tugging at the roots of my hair, spitting and hissing, in Swedish and German and French.

For a full minute I battled with her, first punching her ample solar plexus, then between her legs, all the while trying to inject her in various parts, when all at once she tore away from me and threw herself upon Varda, who was for some reason struggling with the little girl.

"My angel!" the nurse screeched in German. "No-one is going to take you if I—"

Varda let go of the girl and grabbed the nurse by the hair, and in a second had her on the sidewalk in a reverse Nelson. I wanted to shout at her, to tell her to go easy, but I had no time to talk, because right then two little girls in lace-trimmed black dresses raced past me, screeching, and as one tripped, both of them fell upon each other and somehow got tangled between my legs, just as I was trying to hoist Léon on my shoulder.

I was knocked down again, with Léon on top of me; and as I kept trying to peer from between the skinny white socks dancing and scampering before my eyes, with Léon's blood dripping on my eyebrows, I saw the nurse lying on the sidewalk, like a large blonde chicken with neck bent sideways, oddly elongated.

Varda's pink face swam into my view. "I had to!" she screeched. "I had to!"

"Get into the van and let's go!" I said, struggling again to my feet, feeling Léon's blood dripping on my neck.

But Varda was already gone, racing toward avenue Foch, Gross's little girl dragging behind her, legs akimbo.

"Mathilde!" I hollered. (This was Varda's codename). "Mathilde! Let's go!"

But she kept running, dragging the girl behind her.

"*Halt!*" she shouted at Gross in German, and I saw that she had grabbed his little niece by the throat, with her own *katsa* knife under the little ear. "Come back, you fucker!"

Madness!

Through Léon's blood I saw Varda jerking the little girl's head back, the white neck arching upwards.

Madness! Madness! One look at a Nazi, and we forgot everything. Everything!

Then, as in a slow dream, I saw that the girl was not Gross's niece at all, but one of the other girls, which Varda had grabbed by mistake. The girl's eyes, frozen with terror, looked up into Varda's chin, as if something was growing out of it.

I wanted to shout, to tell Varda that she had got the wrong girl, that she had made a dreadful error, that The Smiler would never come back for a stranger, that the flics would be upon us in a second, but an invisible fist seemed to have been rammed down my throat and not a word came out.

"Halt!" Varda screamed across the avenue. "*Ha-a-lt!*"

Then, to my dull astonishment, as in a silent movie, I saw Gross halt in mid-stride.

He turned around, honking cars flowing to his right and left, like water unfurling before a reed growing in the Yarkon River, and for a brief second he looked at Varda, then at me, smiling crookedly.

"*Haaalt!*" Varda howled, in a voice like an animal's, "Come heeere!"

Madness!

As I tugged my Beretta out of its plastic holster at the small of my back and hoisted it up, Gross kept staring at me with that peculiar little smile. Then his smile widened and softened and turned radiant. And as Varda's knife began to move, I felt my bladder loosen; and all at once, with my index finger already searching for the soft trigger-spot, I found myself hoping that the man floating in the V of my gunsight would dash away from me, hoping beyond hope.

Terror

Every child in Ibn Gabirol Street came to watch, from a prudent distance, as my brother and Chaim Shlein, his erstwhile friend, stood forehead to forehead under the old mulberry tree, tears trickling down their noses, shouting curses at each other in Arabic and Hebrew and Yiddish.

It had started (no-one remembers how) as an ordinary brawl, but soon escalated into a contest of Arab curses, complete with the obscene Arab gesture of *zayin*, and finally soared into the realm of derisive chants.

Perhaps because Chaim Shlein had begun to chant in Arabic about our mother's game leg (a chant in which all the other children gleefully joined), or maybe because Ruthy Levin, too, had joined in the chant, all at once my brother gave a mad scream, like a rooster being slaughtered, grabbed two fistfuls of quicklime from the pile before House No. 9, and ground them into Chaim's eyes, thoroughly and at length.

Piles of quicklime were then abundant on Ibn Gabirol Street, which, like the rest of Tel Aviv, resembled a huge construction site with communal apartment houses sprouting everywhere to house the Jews who had been liberated from the camps. This, in fact, was how we children used to classify our parents, by their camp of origin: Ruthy's parents were from Dachau; my own parents have come from Auschwitz (where they had met in unspecified circumstances—something to do with an apple core); Chaim's mother, like all those from House No. 12, was from Treblinka; but before that day, no-one had ever seen her: Chaim's father (also from Treblinka) was the one who did their shopping. He also hung their laundry on the roof. His mother just stayed home all day, and played the piano, but Chaim's screams had brought her down for the first time: a thin balding woman with a flattened nose, her long yellow dress flapping at her ankles as she ran awkwardly, shouting in glottal German.

Five sworn enemies of my brother instantly informed her of what he had just done to her only son. Hissing like a tzefa snake, she snatched a piece of construction lumber, and, ignoring Chaim entirely, lashed at my brother's legs, his back, and, as hysteria gripped her, also his head. He was five years old at the time.

In a moment a circle formed around them, chanting and clapping: *Serves you right! Serves you right!*

As my brother writhed on the ground, trying to shield his head against the blows, the chanting rose in volume and in pitch, drowning out his screams. And as I felt my bladder loosen in terror and self-pity and shame, I too joined in the chant. Yes, I too joined in.

Three wars and 40 years later I can still remember it: the cold quaver behind my belly button, the trickle of warm pee on my thigh, the pain in my palms as I slapped them together and screamed out the words, louder than anyone else, in terror that the she-demon might take it into her head that I, too, was connected with her victim; or, worse, that I was about to come to his aid.

So I clapped and chanted, chanted and clapped.

Serves you right! Serves you right!

Forty years later, I can still remember it all: the sour smell of the quicklime, and my urine; Mrs. Shlein's bony shoulders rising and falling with the blows; her sharp hips swaying under the yellow dress; the thin ankles stomping on the white gravelly lime; and, under the repeated arcs of the grey stick, my little brother rolling from side to side, his bloodied hands raised over his head, and his eyes, pink with terror, staring at me with slowly dying hope.

My parents had just moved to Ibn Gabirol Street the month before. It was, at the time, a new section in north Tel Aviv, rising from among the old shacks, dung filled mule-stables, and scraggly orchards, now destined for uprooting, that had once been the neighbouring Arab village of Sumeil. Only six years before, the Arabs had used it as a base for car bombs, snipers and other acts of terror, until the Haganah cleaned it out, in one night. My father, already a platoon commander in '48, a mere three years after he had arrived in Palestine, helped lead the attack.

With their orchards gone, surly young Arabs worked in construction, on Ibn Gabirol Street, for five *lirot* a day, often sleeping where they worked, on the gravelly grounds, wrapped in burlap sacks. They were wiry and brooding and dark, and their clothes stank. Everyone feared them. Some of them stole laundry; others urinated in doorways. No-one knew what they might do.

One of them, a tall fellow with half his teeth missing, now grabbed Chaim and dunked his head in a pail of water, to wash out his eyes. This, most likely, was what saved his eyesight. But what saved my brother—and me, too, perhaps—was my mother, who suddenly materialized in a flash of white legs and blue-black eyes. In complete silence she tore the board from Mrs. Shlein's thin hand and flung it astonishingly far. She then slapped her face twice, and, still saying not a word, picked up my bloodied brother and limped up the stairs, home.

Many years later, just before she at last died of her cancer, I asked her what she had felt at that moment, when she saw me standing there, clapping along with my brother's enemies. She did not reply (she was going in and out of coma), and I did not ask her again. What else could she have felt but contempt for her coward of a son?

Perhaps (I do hope so) she did not even hear my question; maybe this was why I had waited so long to ask it. Or perhaps I had waited until she had suffered too, before I had allowed her to judge me.

How odd it sounds, now. *Waited for her to suffer too*, she who had come from that other planet. But then, who can foretell all the means we employ to absolve ourselves, to deceive ourselves, and also others.

That evening, when he came home from his army base and heard what had happened, my father came into my room and slowly and wordlessly peeled down my pants; then, holding his soft commando boot by its tip, he thrashed my buttocks for a full five minutes, in silent fury, until finally my mother, who had been feeding my brother chicken broth in the kitchen, called out weakly and asked him to stop.

Only years later, when I, too, began to read newspapers, did I learn that, the night before, my father had taken his *Sayeret* platoon—the recon commando—across the border to Qalqilya, in

Jordan, to blow up nine houses where Arab terrorists lived, in retribution for the attack on a kindergarten in Rosh Ha'Ayin the week before. This attack on Qalqilya was the first retribution operation ever. Five of my father's soldiers had been killed that night, two of them childhood friends from Poland who had come out of Auschwitz with him in '45. Two of the others were from Dachau; the fifth was from Haifa, a *sabra*.

Much later still, after I had joined the Mossad and had access to the files, I learned that there was a stink about the operation, when a few leftist kibbutznik ministers discovered that some women and children were also killed in Qalqilya, when their houses were blown up—they hadn't obeyed the order to leave, or something. But the stink died down quickly. In the kindergarten in Rosh Ha'Ayin, five children had been slaughtered by the terrorists, three of them with knives.

At the time I didn't know all this. I only saw that this was not the father I knew. (Before that day he had never beaten me, nor my brother, ever.) Today I would like to think that he had hit me not only because of my cowardice, but also because of this fresh horror he'd just come back from; or maybe because he was tired—he had not slept for 48 hours, perhaps more (they had to go back, to extricate two *Sayeret* guys who had lost their way, in some *wadi*.)

The shock of the beating, as much as my shame, made me cry with such abandon that I felt myself turning blue. Yet my father did not relent, nor did he try to comfort me. This, perhaps more than the beating itself, magnified my terror. At last, after my mother called to him from the kitchen a second time, my father let me pull up my pants, and in a voice terrible in its evenness, said to me, "Never, but never, take someone else's side against your own brother."

My terror and shame had coalesced by then into a ball of warm hysteria, nearly dreamlike in its intensity, and I found myself groping for a reason, something besides fear, anything, that I could cite to justify myself.

"But he deserved it!" I screamed. "He almost blinded Chaim! He was to blame! He deserved it! He—"

A huge slap stopped me in mid-word, the blue numbers appearing and vanishing in a flash. "He's your brother!" my father said into my face from up close. "No matter what he does, he's your brother."

By now I had convinced myself that this, indeed, was why I had deserted my brother. "So what if he's my brother?" I howled. "He could have burnt the eyes of—"

"Doesn't matter what he did. He's your brother. Family comes first."

"Before justice?" I screeched.

"Before everything."

This simple rule, that family comes first—before justice, before fear—possessed me from that moment for the rest of my life—that, and the lasting shame of having abandoned my brother to his enemies because of cowardice. And somehow, in that strange way the soul has of repairing itself, over time I even managed to convince myself that my cowardice had really been a manifestation of my precocious sense of justice—indeed, had been born of it. For did not my brother commit a crime? If not for the quick dunking in that pail of water, Chaim Shlein would have lost his eyesight. That he had not, did not diminish my brother's sin one bit. He had sinned, and I, his brother, had put justice before family feelings. Was I wrong? Perhaps a little; but not entirely. Guilty of misguided idealism, perhaps. But not dishonourably so.

For a long time I even believed this. And yet, oddly, instead of becoming a perverted justice-seeker, as my brother did, later defending some of the worst terrorists before the Israeli High Court for no fee, I always came back to my father's simple rule: Is it good for my family, for my friends, for those I love? And as I grew older, the question simply became: Is it good for my people? Is it good for my own folk?

I remember how vividly it all came back, years later, when I heard Raymond Aron, the French intellectual, speak on television. Until his mother was killed by a bomb in an Algerian *souk* in '54, he had been agitating for Algerian independence, and at a great personal cost: he was passed over for election to the Académie (only in '64 did he finally become a member, in the teeth of bitter personal interventions by Sartre and Mauriac); he was fired from his job as a broadcast commentator; and his books were not reprinted. The day after his mother's funeral, however, Aron's politics changed diametrically. Many of his new views were not even printable, so virulent had they become.

He was already an old man when I saw him on television in Paris, in a small hotel-room in the *dix-neuvième*, where I was lying low for couple of days, after a take-down for the Mossad. I think it was on "Apostrophes," that wonderful literary talk show, that I saw him. His latest book, *Mémoires*, had just climbed to the top of the bestseller list.

A leftist journalist from *Le Monde* asked Aron bitingly (I no longer remember apropos of what, perhaps to score a moral point) to explain his curious change of view.

Aron replied in an even voice: "*J'aime la justice, mai ma mère j'aime mieux.*"

I was very drunk. The job had nearly gone badly: we were after a PLO shawish who had masterminded the hijacking of two El Al planes, as well as a machine-gun attack on a third, in Munich, where eleven Jews were killed. He had arrived in Paris for a meeting with the PLO executive; we had learned of it by accident. But someone (perhaps the local tailers) must have screwed up along the way, because when we burst into his apartment in the *seiz-ième*, there was an enormously fat woman at his side, her yellow *combinaison* raised above her knees—probably a hooker he had picked up somewhere—and she stupidly tried to defend him (maybe she was Arab too), with that straight razor that nearly all Parisian hookers carry. While we were grappling with her, idiotically, the *shawish* almost got away. Finally we finished them both.

My Number Two and Three were now sleeping in the other room, snoring. I don't know why, but I picked up the phone and called my brother in Tel Aviv, to yak, going through one of our Zurich numbers, just in case the DST computers were already combing the switchboards for all calls to Israel. In Tel Aviv the time was perhaps three in the morning.

He was not surprised to hear my call. I used to call him like this from all over, at odd hours. After my divorce from Ruthy he had become my base, so to speak. He didn't mind; or if he did, he never said so. We talked at length: about father (like Begin, he had recently become a recluse), my brother's work, politics, old tales from Ibn Gabirol Street, this and that. We talked maybe half an hour. What the hell, the Mossad was paying. Just before we hung up, I said for no reason at all that I was sorry I hadn't tried to beat up Mrs. Shlein that day.

"Beat up who?" said my brother.

I reminded him of the event, in some detail.

"I can't remember," he said, and indeed I could see that he did not.

After we hung up, I couldn't sleep. Somehow his forgetfulness filled me with anger, as if I had just been robbed of something, not absolved of a sin. I had long ago realized that it was Mrs. Shlein I had been trying to kill, all these years, not just my people's enemies. So my brother's forgetfulness should have been a relief to me; I don't know why it wasn't.

Anyway, I am not ashamed of all I have done. I am not proud either, although my father is (I know, since he's told me so himself), and so, in an odd way, is my brother. "Someone has to do it," he said to me once, after he had won the release of some bastards it had taken us two years to catch, "so the rest of us can live quietly. What does the motive matter?"

Maybe it doesn't. But lately I have begun to think of my father's motive. Did he have a Mrs. Shlein too, in his past, on that other planet? I know I will never have the courage to ask him.

Test

What I want to tell about happened on the last day of my *katsa* Tests, in the final exercise. We were supposed to simulate a take-down, go through all the steps, but then do only as-if. We had done similar exercises before, during the course, both on the Mossad's premises and off, but this was part of the Authorization Tests, so we paid extra attention; me especially, because with a father who had once been 2IC to the first *Memuneh*, and had helped catch Eichmann, and everything, I had no intention of fucking up.

Now, the man whose take-down we were supposed to fake was just an old retired beadle, living on the corner of Achad Ha'Am and Lillienblum; I think they had chosen him (he of course knew nothing about it) because he stayed mostly at home, and went out only to buy groceries and newspapers, every two or three days, with no fixed routine, so this of course made the take-down tougher to plan. But after four days of recon, Yossi Gellerman, my Number Two, finally discovered that, every morning, after this beadle guy woke up, he passed by his window with his phylacteries on—probably going for his morning prayers in the enclosed kitchen terrace (it faced east, toward Jerusalem); so this would be our chance. The only thing was, he would be visible for only five, maybe six seconds, but you don't need much time for this anyway. Two seconds to aim the Anschutz, two more to get the crosshairs on him, one second to press the trigger—five seconds tops. And just because it was going to be an as-if, and the Anschutz would have only a camera inside its barrel, not a bullet, did not mean it would be easy, just the opposite, because with a camera you have to hold the rifle extra steady or the picture comes out all fuzzy, and then who knows if they'll pass you.

"Oh, don't worry, I'll put it right between his eyes," Yossi Gellerman said, after I had warned him for the fifth time not to screw up.

"Eye, ear, nose," I said, "I don't give a *zayin* where. Just do him, so we can go get some falafel."

My stomach was rumbling something awful, because I hadn't eaten anything since the previous night, to keep my senses sharp, like we'd been taught.

"Don't you worry," Yossi said. "I'll get him." He himself had eaten a full breakfast, and now lay on his back, the Anschutz on his stomach, smoking a Dubek cigarette.

"Want one?" he said, blowing smoke at me.

"You just watch the fucking window," I said.

We were lying, the two of us, on the floor of a grungy terrace in Lillienblum Street, three floors up, waiting for this beadle guy to appear. The owner of the apartment was in Tveriah, in a convalescence home, so we knew we would be safe. Also, this was a Friday morning, when Lillienblum Street is especially quiet, because all the old men who live there go to the Rothschild

Boulevard parliament, to sit on the benches and debate the burning issues of the day.

I was just beginning to debate with myself whether to take a cigarette from Yossi, or just bum a drag from his, when from the apartment above us came a sort of moan.

"Did you hear that?" Yossi said. "This sound."

"What sound? It's the wind," I said.

As far as we knew, the building was empty—not that it mattered, because if this take-down was for real, the Anschutz would have been silenced with a three-incher, and no-one would hear a thing; still, you don't want to have people around you, in this, in case something gets fucked up and you have to scoot.

"No, listen," Yossi said. "Here it is again."

And indeed, there it was, a sort of a soft cry.

"Probably just some cats screwing," I said.

Tel Aviv is full of cats, and that's the only thing they do all day, screwing, making more cats. Just like Arabs.

"No, it's not a cat," Yossi said. "It's someone, he's sick or something, I am telling you."

"So what do you want me to do?" I said. "So he's sick."

I couldn't believe it. Ten seconds to take-down, and he becomes a doctor.

But Yossi would not let off. "Hell, no," he said. "It's a woman. Listen, listen!"

"Yeah," I said. "So it's a woman. Probably a whore who went up on the roof with a client, to the laundry-room. You never heard a woman getting it, before?"

Laundry-rooms on roofs were notorious for assignations. High-school students usually went up there, to screw, so almost every such place had a mattress.

"A whore?" Yossi said. "Friday morning? Here?"

It was true. Hookers usually worked only Friday nights and Saturdays; and they only worked in Herzl Street, not on Achad Ha'Am, where the only people living were 80-year-old Second Immigration farts.

"So maybe she started early," I said, keeping my eye on the window below. "She owed her pimp money, something."

But the moans now rose in volume, and I myself began to feel uneasy. Because what if someone on the street heard and came up to the laundry-room, to investigate? Yossi and I would be visible like fish on the beach, with the Anschutz and everything.

"Forget the whore," I snapped at him. "It's less then a minute now, so let's do it and—"

Just then the woman gave out an ululation, like a Moroccan bridesmaid, and Yossi thumped his fist on the floor. "That's not a whore! I am telling you, it's someone, she's having a baby, right over our heads! How did she get in there?"

I snarled at him that I didn't know and didn't care, and fuck me if I was going to blow my Tests because of some whore who had forgotten to count the days. "First Rule," I said. "Remember? The job comes first, and nothing comes second! First Rule!"

But Yossi was only listening to the moans now. "Maybe she's someone's daughter, grand-daughter, what do I know, and she came to visit her grandma, something? You think we should call her an ambulance? After we finish?"

I began to tell him that for all I cared she could do it all by her-self, like the *Arabushot* do it in the fields, but at that moment I saw something move in the window below. So I grabbed Yossi's hip and flatted him on the floor. "Here he comes. Now I want a good picture, with the phylacteries in the centre. You hear?"

Yossi began to aim. "But we can call an ambulance, after we finish. No? Just before we leave—"

"Yeah, sure," I said. "Maybe call the police too? And the firemen? Then if something gets really fucked up—"

At that moment the woman began to scream. I am telling you, it was awful, the way she hollered, as if someone was cutting her throat; that the baby was stuck, that she could see its legs; that please, please someone call a doctor.

I began to plug my ears; and just then the beadle leaned out the window. Probably to see where the screams were coming from. I couldn't believe our luck. A perfect shot. Perfect! But Yossi, this idiot, had gotten up from the floor. "I can't aim with this noise anyway," he said.

I called after him not be a donkey, to come back, but he went in anyway and phoned *Hadassah* hospital, and five minutes later came a white Subaru, with its windows curtained, with the *Memuneh* himself inside, and his 2IC, and they took both Yossi and me and the woman back to Glilott, where they paraded the three of us in front of the entire *katsa* course, and then the 2IC told Yossi to pack his stuff and fuck off. Because of course this woman (her name was Varda, an embassy *katsa* from Paris, on a homeland visit) was only a decoy, to tempt us, to see what we would do.

"So take an example," the *Memuneh* said. "When you are on a job, nothing should take your mind away from it. Nothing." He went on to speak about King Shaul, and how he lost his kingdom because he had not followed God's orders to slay the captive king Aggag and exterminate all the Amalekites. "And all because of pity," the *Memuneh* ended. "So remember it, once you get your Authorizations. When you come here, leave your pity at home, so that louses like Gellerman can afford to have theirs."

I don't think any one of us ever forgot this. Only much later, when I was five years *katsa* already, did my father tell me that they do it to every course, they always set up someone to fuck up like this, as an example.

Now why am I telling you this? Because last year, when I was commander of the *katsa* course (this was one year before my retirement), no-one fucked up, in the Tests. Not one. For a while I thought of asking for a volunteer, in secret, someone who would feign a fuck-up, for instructional purposes. But when I talked to my father he said I should lay off, because maybe the Jews had learned their lesson, and there was no more need for this Test anymore. I said I doubted it; but the following year, the same thing happened again, no-one fucked up. So this part of the Tests was then abolished.

Black

My father's cousin Baruch who worked as a butcher in Tel Aviv's Carmel market, married a Moroccan cleaning-woman seven years older, and was immediately cut off from the family. Not because she was older—my own mother is four years older than my father—nor because she was a cleaning-woman—my father, after all, was a balegooleh, a mule driver—but because she was a Schwartze, black; a Moroccan Jewess. Her name was Pirchiyah Azoulai, and as a matter of fact she was born in Israel, but the rest of her family had come from Fez, in the Atlas mountains in Morocco. So that's what they were. In Israel they lived in a small village near Be'er Sheva, where Pirchiyah's father, Leon Azoulai, was a lay Rabbi, and her mother, Freha, a spell-woman who, so it was said, still did Moroccan black-magic on the side. But one of Pirchiyah's sisters had married an army paratroop major, and a brother of hers worked in the Interior Ministry as assistant Kashrut inspector. Still, she was a Moroccan, a Schwartze, and we, Ashkenazi, white. What's more, my own grandfather,

Yechezke'el Leib Zalmanovitch (after whom I am named), a bale-gooleh like my father, had been an early disciple of the first Boyberishe Rebbe, whom he used to drive to Polish villages to waken up slumbering Jewish souls; and my mother, though a daughter of a fish-grocer from Krakow, was from her side also not without distinction: her grandfather, Moshe-Chaim Bloom, a bookbinder, had once visited the Holy Ari of Safed, the great Kabbalist, and later wrote a match-making guide with simple spells from the Kabbalah (which my mother claims she had learned at his knee).

A Moroccan in our family was clearly out of the question.

"We have Yechezke'el to think of," my father said.

In secret, though, my mother still went to see Baruch, in his butcher-shop in the Carmel market, and occasionally even bought from him a beef shank, or a plucked chicken. But neither he nor his wife were invited to weddings, circumcisions or Bar Mitzvahs.

"Or we'd have to invite them all," said my father.

At first Baruch said he didn't care. "You don't want me, fine. I'll go to hers." Meaning Pirchiyah's family. But after a few years, most likely prodded by his wife, who in the meantime had borne him four children, he came one day to our apartment on Bazel Street and said to my father, "Listen. Me, all right. Keep out if you want. But my children, invite them at least? What have they sinned, that they can't sit with their family? They are his cousins!" Meaning mine.

"You should have thought of it before," said my father.

Now all this took place in 1970, just before my own Bar Mitzvah, which was supposed to be a big thing—I had just had a bout with scarlatina, when my father made a vow before the Holy Ark to spend 1,000 *Lirot* on the festivity, if I recovered. When I did, my mother rented the largest hall under the Maxim cinema, and engaged rabbi Simcha Tuvim of the Bugrashov synagogue to teach me the reading of the Torah. (It was the Scroll of Eicha, I recall, where the Maiden of Zion is consoled by the prophet, Yechezke'el, who tells her that one day it will all be set aright.) All my father's cousins from Canada and New York were invited, and my mother's family from Bney Barak, although the balegooleh friends of my father were not. (My father had stopped driving a cart the year before, and now had three carts, which he rented out to others.) Every day I practiced my Reading, and also a Kreizler sonata on my violin, for the guests. Once a week I went to Nachum Litvak the tailor, to have my measurements re-taken, for my first long pants and jacket; and gifts began arriving: a Motorola transistor radio from America, and, from Canada, an Omega wristwatch with seventeen stones and a wallet with thirteen Canadian dollars in it, in bills of fives and ones. Then my father, one week before the Torah Reading, took me to Kalman's bicycle store on the corner of Bar Cochba and Dizzengoff, and let me pick a three-speed red Raleigh, with a tilting seat, and after he had paid, marched me to Bergman's kiosk across the street, had Yossef Bergman place two chairs on the sidewalk, and ordered two coffees—one for him, one for me. It was my first.

"You are going to be a mensch soon," my father said, slurping his coffee, which he drank with lots of milk.

"Sure," I said, slurping mine proudly.

Everything seemed set. Even my violin no longer squeaked in the last part of the sonata. Then one week before my Bar Mitzvah, Pirchiyah came to see my father.

It was a Friday eve when she arrived, and we had already finished the Shabbat meal. My mother had washed the dishes, and my father, wearing an apron, was drying them at the sink when Pirchiyah knocked on the door, and without waiting for an answer, entered. Her long hair was loose, she wore purple trousers and gave off a strong smell of soap.

"I want to talk to you," she said to my father.

My mother looked at her, then at my father, and wrung her hands.

My father said, "Not in front of the child."

"Yes in front," said Pirchiyah. "Why not? Let him know."

"I beg of you," said my mother.

"Out," said my father, extending his hand in a gesture of divine expulsion. "Out of my house!"

"Shmiel," said my mother. "Let her speak at least."

"Speak what?"

"I have a message," said Pirchiyah. "From my mother."

"A message? So rejoice!" said my father. "A message from the *machasheyfa*."

The last word he said in Yiddish; it means both a witch and a shrew.

"I beg of you," my mother said again, not making clear whether she had meant Pirchiyah, my father, or both.

Pirchiyah said, "And if you don't, you'll see."

There was a short pause. My mother said, "All the invitations are already—"

"Not for me," said Pirchiyah, "for them."

And one by one, from behind her, the four children filed in: handsome and odd-looking, the two boys with Pirchiyah's tight curly hair but Baruch's fair skin, the two girls with dark skin and blond tresses.

They stood by the wall, in a line, as if they had practised it.

"So what will she do?" said my father. "Bring up Ashmedai?" He laughed out loud.

"Please, Shmiel!" cried my mother.

My father said, "I'm a balegooleh, not a Moroccan."

There was a tense pause. Pirchiyah's face contorted. At first I thought she would shout, or argue, or cry, but she did none of these things. Instead, from a pocket in her pants she pulled out a little jar, and unscrewed the top.

"What—" my father began, then he jumped to push me away, but it was too late. Pirchiyah had sprinkled the jar's contents on me—it was either blood (chicken's, probably), or some other thick liquid—and recited quickly something in a high-pitched voice.

My mother screamed.

"If my children can't be there," hissed Pirchiyah, "then neither will he," and one by one she and her children filed out, the eldest daughter bringing up the rear.

My father rushed to the hall, and shouted after them, that she should stay in the Carmel market, with the rest of the Schwartzes, not come to his home to do dirty Moroccan black magic. "Not even for a Shiv'a!" he hollered. "You hear? Not even for a Shiv'a!"

The stink of the red liquid was so overpowering—it seemed to have stuck to my hair, to my clothes, to my hands—that it took nearly an hour to wash it off. My mother stripped me naked and gave me a long bath, scrubbing me with a fresh luffa, crying all the while. I retched twice into the bath-water, and my mother brought me tea, with a spoonful of Carmel benediction wine, which she made me drink even as I sat in the water. Then she tucked me in bed, covering me with her own down blanket.

"Tomorrow you'll forget about it," she said, still crying. "You'll see."

But the next day I came down with fever. Dr. Gottlieb came to the house, and said there was a chance the scarlatina would return.

"Just keep him in bed," he said, "and plenty of tea."

"It's not scarlatina!" my mother wailed, when he had left. "It's from her!—Shmiel—go to her, beg her pardon—"

"Never in the world," said my father, adding inexplicably, "you want maybe to give the land back to the Arabs also?"

My mother grabbed his shirt. "You want your son to read the Torah next week? Yes or no."

"He'll read," said my father. "He'll read. With 40 degrees fever he'll read!"

But that afternoon my fever soared above 41 degrees, and I was rushed to *Hadassah* hospital. My father drove me there himself, in a cart hitched to his best mule.

"You stay with him," said my mother, "in case she comes back."

Both ended staying, sitting by my bedside.

That night I became delirious. Black soldiers with enormous shoes emerged from under my bed, marching straight into the wall where they were swallowed by a red mouth ringed by black eyes. The ceiling, its rim fading into dark nothingness, rotated viciously, first one way, then another. I woke up to see two nurses pressing socks with crushed ice to my forehead and neck. A doctor pushed a swab down my throat, then made me swallow a large sulfa capsule.

The next two days I received more sulfa, and injections. Rabbi Simcha Tuvim came to my bedside, wrapped in a prayer shawl, and said Tehillim over me, staring into the wall.

In spite of the sulfa, my fever lingered. The Bar Mitzvah had to be postponed.

"Go to her, Shmiel!" my mother wailed. "Ask her to come!"

"Never!"

"Don't be a mule!"

"No!"

My mother grabbed his hand. "If we cancel," she cried, "it'll cost 700 *lirot*. At least!"

My father put a fresh ice-filled sock on my forehead.

My mother went on, "The family will go back to Canada, and America—"

"No! I said no!"

"Then next month we'll have to do it only with the bale-goolehs—"

There was a long silence.

My father stood up.

"All right," he rasped, his cheeks dark. "But I'm doing it for you!"

My mother sobbed. "And for him?"

"For you only," said my father, not looking at me. "When he grows up and goes to the army he'll understand."

I couldn't see what the army had to do with it; but many things I did not understand then.

That evening Pirchiyah came to the hospital, Baruch silent at her side. He remained standing, while she sat at my bedside, and touched my forehead with a hand smelling of laundry soap.

"How are you, Yechezke'el?" Her voice was guttural, the glottals as deep as those of a radio announcer.

I swallowed through my constricted throat.

"Fine . . ." I croaked.

"Here, swallow this—" and before my mother could stop her, Pirchiyah had placed a folded piece of paper on my tongue, propped my head with one hand, and brought a glass of water to my lips with the other.

Confused, I swallowed.

My mother grabbed my chin, forcing my mouth open. But the paper had gone down already.

"What is it?" she shouted.

"An amulet," said Pirchiyah, "from her."

My mother said, "Aren't you ashamed of what you've done to him?"

Pirchiyah said, "What you want for him, I want for mine."

"This we shall see," said my mother.

There was a pause.

My father said, "I already invited them—"

"So you invited," said my mother.

That night my fever broke. My Bar Mitzvah had been postponed, but only by one week—most of my father's Canadian and American cousins remained, only three had left, and my father invited three balegoolehs in their place. He also invited Baruch and Pirchiyah, and their children, and Pirchiyah's parents.

It was the first time that I had seen them: Pirchiyah's mother was an enormously fat woman in a flowery dress, with black eyes rimmed with red, and a faint plume of a moustache, who sat in her corner the entire evening and knitted skullcaps. Pirchiyah's father was as small as a Yemenite, with a scraggly beard and a thin hook nose. Not once did I see him raise his eyes—he just ate and ate. Pirchiyah and Baruch ate nothing—they just danced to the Kleizmer music, non-stop. But their children did eat, all except the eldest (whose name, I later learned, was Sarina) who sat between her grandparents, placid and observant like her grandmother, staring at me keenly all the while (my cheeks slowly heating under her gaze), as I thanked my father and mother in a speech, as I played the violin, as I later sat and ate double and triple helpings.

But just as I was about to launch into the compote, she suddenly rose to her feet, came up to our table, and asked if she could sit beside me.

My mother smiled at her thinly. "Why?" she asked.

"Because when I grow up I'll marry him."

My mother's smile disappeared.

I looked up in confusion, my heart seizing with wild heat. "Me?" I asked. "Why?"

"Because you are for me." She quickly sat down beside me, took out a folded paper packet, and sprinkled some powder on my compote bowl, which I was then raising to my lips. "Drink it."

"No!" cried my mother. "No!"

But it was too late—I had drunk up, quickly, and Sarina had left to join her grandmother, who now raised her eyes and gave me a large warm smile.

My mother then did something I'll never forget.

In front of everyone, the kleizmer orchestra, the waiters, my father's American and Canadian cousins, her own family from Bney Barak, she grabbed my head, clamped it under her armpit, forced my mouth open with her thumbs, and stuck two fingers down my throat.

"Out with it!" she hissed into my face. "All of it!"

I struggled—the fingers digging into my throat were like hot snakes—but my head seemed stuck in concrete. Helplessly I vomited, throwing up the chicken gizzards, the gefilte fish, the soup, the calf tongue in tomato sauce, the prune compote. I threw up on the table, upon my mother's new pink dress, on my father's blue suit—he just sat there, unmoving—and on my own.

When I finished retching, my mother gave me a glass of water.

"Now drink," she said, not even looking at me.

All dancing, all music, all talking, every movement or sound in the hall, had stopped. There was an odd, tingling silence, broken by my sobs.

Then, across the room, Pirchiyah's mother folded her knitting and slowly stood up; and right after her, Pirchiyah's father, then Baruch and Pirchiyah herself, and the children.

Pirchiyah's grandmother opened her mouth to speak, but no voice came out.

My mother was staring at her with eyes as black and red-rimmed as hers.

"Not in my home," she said. "Out!"

And that was it. A year later Baruch and Pirchiyah left Tel Aviv, with the children, and went to live in Dimonah, where Baruch went to work for HaMashbir, as a food clerk, while Pirchiyah found work as a cook in the Nuclear reactor, or perhaps in the Hawk missile battery guarding it. I no longer remember. No-one in the family talked to either of them much, though I once saw Pirchiyah with her daughter in Tel Aviv, coming out of a cheap clothing store—I think the daughter was Sarina. She had grown very tall—taller than me, and, like her grandmother, had large black eyes and a faint moustache; but this, like her long blond hair, seemed oddly out of place on her dark-olive skin. She looked at me without recognition while I nodded at her mother.

I was about to go into cinema Yaron, with Nurit, my then girl-friend, when I saw them. I was in my Air Force uniform, a pilot cadet, and very proud of it.

"Who's she?" asked Nurit, not making clear whether she had meant Pirchiyah, or her daughter.

"Used to be our cleaning lady," I said. "In Bazel Street."

To my surprise I felt neither guilt nor shame at the lie. And this was strange, because I had always thought of myself as free from prejudice.

Life in Parts

When my father-in-law took me for the first time to a whorehouse I was married barely two years.

"Don't be afraid," he said to me, peeling four 1000-franc notes and slipping them into the blue porcelain bowl in the entrance. "Jews don't come here, ordinarily. Nobody will know." When I foolishly put my hand to my hip pocket, he pursed his lips and closed both eyes, giving his palms and head a fast shake, in that French moue meaning, "This one is on me."

We were passing through Paris, he and I, on the way back to Tel Aviv from Zurich, where he had taken me to introduce me to the Swiss banker that for the last 23 years had kept his account. "In case something happens," he said. "I don't want her involved." Meaning his wife.

Every year he has visited his banker, in Zurich, and on the way back passed through Paris. Up to now I had thought he did it for the food.

I myself used to live in Paris until two years previously, when

I had met his daughter at a party in Neuilly (she was a swimsuit model for Gotex, the Israeli fashion firm) and went back with her to my tiny room on avenue Voltaire. I had been foolishly trying to become a painter for more than a year, but after two days of trying to paint her in the nude I became convinced I would never be one. Somehow I kept missing something, perhaps in her skin, perhaps in her face.

"So let's get married," she said, hugging a towel over her breasts, as she sat hunched on my narrow bed, "and then you could paint me every day, if you want, after work."

When I hesitated, she said, "You could also speak French with my father. He speaks French."

Her father had been born in Marseille, to a Rabbinical family who all later perished in the Molech's maw; but as he had left home early to ride horses in Auteuil (the first Jewish jockey ever, I am told), pretending to be a goy, he was spared. Later he joined the Resistance, helping General Boca in the Maquis, and after the war ended hunted a few Nazis, on his own, before coming to Israel, where he helped start the Tel Aviv stock exchange and launch three small conglomerates.

He was already retired, when I married his daughter and reluctantly returned to Tel Aviv to work in advertising and do reserve service. We never talked much, he and I, but after his first heart attack he called me and said he must take me to Zurich, to show me a few things.

"You can take a week off?" he asked.

"Yes, I think so," I said.

He had gotten me the job, when I came back, through his stock exchange connections. I didn't earn much yet, but I worked nights and so had good prospects.

"I'll talk to Shaike," he said.

Shaike was my boss.

"No," I said. "I'll talk to him."

There was a little pause.

"And from there we'll go through Paris," my father-in-law went on, "to eat something, maybe also look around. You like Paris?"

"Yes, sure," I said, recalling the food.

But I hadn't banked on this.

For a full minute I remained standing outside, in the yellow sunshine, while he patiently waited for me to make up my mind.

"Whatever you want," he said.

"All right," I said at last.

The whorehouse was on the ground floor of a grey office building on the good side of avenue Foch, close to the Bois de Boulogne. Inside, it looked like the Zurich private bank we had just visited two days before; but it was better lit, with table-top lamps, not ceiling neons, in the corridor, and Caucasian carpets, not Persian ones. ("Shirvan," my father-in-law said, pointing, "and this is a Daghestan.") The old mustachioed concierge at his formica desk, in front, looked like any gatekeeper at a law firm. He nodded at my father-in-law gravely, greeting him by name.

"A young friend," my father-in-law said, indicating me with his chin.

We stayed till midnight, then returned by taxi to the Hotel Lutèce, where my father-in-law had reserved two rooms already from Tel Aviv. There, too, they seemed to know him. It was a small hotel on the Ile St.-Louis in the middle of the Seine, with a flower-infested courtyard, and narrow rooms with high domed ceilings. It was May, and lilac bloomed everywhere.

"She's like her mother, I am sure," my father-in-law said to me next morning, as we sat at a tiny table on the second floor of

Le Drug Store, at the entrance of the Champs Elysées, dipping croissants in pitch-like coffee. "Frigid. I saw how she walks. A man can tell."

My father-in-law had a theory that men could tell about women, and horses, with a glance. All it took was practice.

I hoisted my shoulder, not denying, not confirming. I had never betrayed my wife before and had never planned to, so the previous night had thrown me into extreme confusion and I hardly knew what to say. But I felt that confirming my father-in-law's suspicions would be going too far.

He went on, speaking into the air alongside my ear, "Her mother, she was always cold." He used the French word, also meaning stuck-up. "I don't know why I love her." Then he levelled his eyes at me. "Believe me, it's better like this, with a pute, not with someone else's wife, or girls from the street. That, no. That is too dangerous."

"O no," I said. "Never."

We were talking in French: he, because he liked it; me, to give him pleasure. Before we had gone on this trip, before his heart attack, we had not talked that often; and when we did, we usually talked in Hebrew.

"That's how it is," my father-in-law said, again talking to the air beside me. "Que voulez vous."

He had ordered a double café-calvados, the small espresso spiked with fiery prune cognac that is the traditional pick-me-up for weary debauchers the morning after. It now arrived, and he tossed it back, quickly.

With his wavy silvery hair and capped teeth he looked like a compact Maurice Chevalier with a Bourville nose. "She is, hein?"

I hoisted my shoulders again, torn between my allegiance to my wife and my debt to the man who had just introduced me to his

Swiss banker and to a five-star whorehouse I could never have discovered on my own, nor afforded.

"Comme-çi, comma-ça," I said at last, looking away.

Outside, on the sidewalk, a clutch of young women passed, laughing musically. One of them waved to someone inside Le Drug Store. Three men waved back. My father-in-law waved too.

"Men and women have only three ways to be compatible," he said, bending his fingers, one by one. "Physical, emotional, intellectual. You can never have all three, never. Two," he raised two bony fingers in a narrow V, "is maximum. This is a proven medical fact, by doctors. Believe me. So which would you give up?"

I said nothing. The fucking of the previous night still reverberated in my spine. I had never had anything like this before in my life, the smoothness, the rhythm, the ease of it. My pute had been a slim short-haired medical student from the Sorbonne, saving her money (so she said) for a flight to Kansas, to visit her boyfriend. "He's in farming," she said. "He grows wheat, barley, also oats. A farmer."

We had already had sex twice (the 2000-francs price was tout compris) but stayed entangled, talking. (We were talking in English, for her benefit: "I have to practice," she said.)

When I said that flights to the US were cheap, that she could probably fly by charter from Brussels for less than 1000 francs, she said she wanted to fly the Concorde, from Paris. "Like a chic movie star, with champagne. Why not? I don't deserve?" Then, perhaps to change the topic, she began to name my muscles, touching them one by one, as if this was a private anatomy lesson. "Deltoid, abdominal rectus, long adductor, sartorius—, no, this is not a muscle. Now the bones: Ilium, sacrum, ischium—, no, no, it is not a bone either—."

Afterwards she gave me a phone number in Kansas, of a message service ("that's the one I call—just say it's for Amande"), in case I ever passed there. "It's far from New York?"

"So so," I said. (I had boasted to her before that I may go to New York on business next year.)

"He lives near Kansas City, with his wife, so I'll have time."

When I left she combed my hair, slicking it with her saliva.

"Me," my father-in-law said into his coffee cup, "at home I want heart and head. This—" he touched his crotch, delicately, "this I can buy outside, everywhere." Then, leaning back in his chair, he began to speak of the account in Zurich, how important it was that I never forgot its number; but I interrupted him and said I did-n't believe there were only three ways for men and women to be compatible.

"Oh yes," he said. "It's well known. Medically."

"Why only three?"

"That's how it is."

Forty years before, after he was done chasing Nazis and just before he left Europe for Palestine, he had studied rhetoric and philosophy for a few months in the Haut Ecole des Sciences Politiques in Paris (as an ancien Maquisard he could study for free). The school was run then by the Jesuits, who, like all true Cartesians, taught him to divide everything in the world into three parts, to grasp it more easily.

This, I have since become convinced, is the secret key to the French national soul: it, too, is divided into three separate parts, none of which ever mixes with the others. In this regard, at least, my father-in-law is a true Frenchman.

"Come," he said. "Let's go eat something good."

The night before, in a small restaurant on the Ile St.-Louis, near the hotel, we had eaten an andouilette: a slice of the large intestine of a cow, well scraped. It had been boiled nearly white and came smeared with a hot Dijon mustard sauce, and was accompanied by snails in garlic butter, but still retained a mild odour of shit.

Only a very few people liked it, my father-in-law explained, so there was a special society for them, the AAAA: L'Association Anonyme d'Amants des Andouilettes. The Anonymous Association of the Lovers of Tripe. He had once been a member, years ago, but had let his membership lapse. Did I like it?

"O yes," I said. "Excellent."

Afterwards we drank a bottle of red Sancerre wine, before going to the whorehouse.

Although we had just finished breakfast, it was time to eat again. Because lunch takes so long in France, it usually starts very early, sometimes as early as 11.30. It was now 11.15, so it was time to get ready.

"What do you want to eat now?" my father-in-law asked. "Before we go see other places."

Our flight to Tel Aviv was due to depart only in the evening, so we had plenty of time.

"Something good," I said.

I vaguely expected to be taken again to some small restaurant, perhaps in the 16e, where all the patrons were old, wore black (and pearls, if they were women), and ate silently and without using the salt shaker. But to my surprise he took me to a boisterous place in the 2e, the Jewish quarter, on the rue des Rosiers.

"Gefilte fish!" he exclaimed, rubbing his hands as we entered. "Like my mother used to make."

Again, to my surprise, he seemed to know quite a number of people, mostly old and wrinkled, and talked to them in a mixture of Yiddish and French. To two of them he brought over a bottle of Carmel Hock, an Israeli wine, again closing his eyes and giving the rapid shake to his head and palms, to indicate that this one was on him.

But coffee we had at the rue du Temple, in a little *patisserie*, and also a few little palmier cookies. "This, the Jews don't know how to make," he said.

By the time we had finished it was mid-afternoon. As we walked outside, in the narrow street, toward the Bourse (he wanted to show me how they traded, but they had just closed for the day), pigeons fluttered above our heads, their wings making an odd clacking sound. Cars honked. Small yellow scooters flitted among the crawling cars.

We were in the 3e, the most ancient part of the Jewish quarter, also called the Shtetl.

"This," my father-in-law pointed, "is where I had my Bar Mitzvah."

It was a nondescript beige house, with a red grill fence. "Used to be a synagogue. The Nazis made it into an officers' club, with women."

I stared at it. An old hag came out, squinted at us, then spit on the sidewalk.

"Everyone came for the Bar Mitzvah," my father-in-law said, ignoring the old woman. "All the family."

I stared at the beige house.

"From Marseille?" I said.

"I was the firstborn," my father-in-law said, as if this explained it.

Without saying anything else he turned on his heels and pulled me away.

At a little café-tabac near the Place de la Concord we had a panaché: a mixture of blond beer and lemonade. "My father taught me to drink it," my father-in-law said. "Used to make the beer himself, so it was glatt Kosher. You like it?"

"Yes," I said.

"My wife, she doesn't like it," my father-in-law said, and ordered another one for me. "But, she's my family now, nu."

All afternoon we strolled. My legs were shaking, but I kept on walking. He seemed like a young man. In the Tuilleries gardens he bought me a cotton candy, as if I was a child.

"So how's work?" he asked me.

I said work was all right.

"You happy?"

"Sure," I lied.

He didn't ask if his daughter was happy. It was her mother's job to ask this.

Three hours before our flight, he said, "Let's go see one more thing, see if it's still there." He snapped his fingers. As if by a miracle, a taxi halted, and we climbed in.

For half an hour we rode it north, saying nothing. At a decrepit cobble-stoned side-street just beyond the Porte de Clignancourt he told the driver to stop.

"Here," he said, pointing with his hand to a crumbling train station. The old metal signs, rusting, drooped over crooked old rails. It was clearly no longer in use. "They left from here."

I didn't have to ask who had left from here.

"Everybody knew, no-one came to give them even a glass of water." He made a half circle with his hand in the air, encompassing the high windows, the grimy rooftops, the hanging laundry. "Nobody." He coughed for a long moment, convulsively.

Then we drove back to the hotel, to pack.

Later that night, on the El Al plane, he said to me, "You take care of her, if something happens, hein?"

I said I would.

He went on, "She never lacked, with me, for anything," not

making clear whether he was speaking of my wife, or of his. "Everything I could give her, I gave." He was speaking of his wife now.

For a while we were quiet; I think he napped a little. I didn't.

Later still, just after the stewardess asked us to buckle our seat-belts (we were about to land in Ben Gurion airport), he suddenly turned to me. "Tell me again, the number. But not loud. In my ear."

As the plane banked, I whispered in his ear the number of the Swiss bank account, very softly.

"Remember!" he said, clutching my hand. "Don't forget!"

"I won't," I said.

The plane banked again, steeply. My father-in-law let go of my hand. Down below, like frozen fields of wheat, the white sand-dunes of the Tel Aviv coast shone at me in the future dark.

Mish-Mash

In 1958 my uncle Nathan Berkovitch married two women and went to live with them both in Haifa until, a year after the weddings, a delegate from Haifa's Rabbinate caught up with him because of an anonymous snitch, and told him he must divorce one of the two or go to jail. Nathan, who was then working as a bookkeeper at the Haifa oil refineries, said he would divorce neither wife, because he loved them both, and what's more, they loved him too; and not only that, but both were pregnant (which was true), and how could you deprive unborn children of a father? Besides, the Yemenite Jews, who just two years before had been brought over to Israel from Yemen in a special operation, half of them had two wives, and not a few (mainly their rabbis) had three, and nobody in the Rabbinate said Boo. So how come? And why did they pester him, Nathan Berkovitch? Just because he was an Ashkenazi Jew? So maybe if he grew curly sidelocks and dyed his skin brown, they'd leave him alone? Huh? Huh?

Now, remember, this was just ten years after the founding of the state of Israel, when no-one made trouble for the authorities—who, as everyone knew, were busy building up the motherland. So Nathan's obstinacy was seen as both a sign of dangerous rebellion and scandalous apostasy. Rebellion, because he refused to do what the Rabbinate—an integral branch of the government—told him; and apostasy, because he claimed that he followed the Bible itself (—where all the patriarchs had more than one wife, and a few had concubines), and not the Bible's explicators and annotators in the Talmud and Mishna—whose opinions counted for him, Nathan, like the skin of an onion. And, he said, it wasn't as if he had a concubine. He had married both his wives legally and openly, before a real rabbi, who, even if he didn't know he was marrying the bridegroom for the second time without a Gett for his first marriage, still was a kosher rabbi, so the marriage held. Besides, the prohibition of multiple wives was not in the Bible, nor in the Talmud, or even in the Mishna. It was merely a thousand-year-old innovation by rabbi Gershom, the Diaspora's Luminescence, the very same one who had forbidden Jews to read letters not addressed to them—a dictum the Rabbinate's hirelings had broken sure as rain, when spying on him, Nathan. So how come the Rabbinate went by one Gerhomite dictum while ignoring the other? Huh? Huh?

All this, and more, Nathan said in the special Rabbinical Court session that he was forced to attend (without his wives). My father, who accompanied him, said that all this threw the Adjudicators for a wide loop. Because, let's face it, according to Jewish religious law, you can't force a man to divorce his wife, even if he's married to a second one. A Gett has to be voluntary on the man's side. If he refuses, you can only throw him in jail until he recants—but if he doesn't want to, you can't do anything, and his wife remains an unmarriageable woman forever. But could you do this here with a clean conscience? I mean, jail? If Nathan went to jail, he would surely lose his job (which, in 1958, was not so easy to come by), and then he couldn't feed his children. So who would feed them? The rabbis, maybe? They hardly had money enough to feed themselves. (This was before the coalition agreement that gave government stipends to all yeshiva students and exempted them from military service.)

And to make matters worse, both Nathan's wives—one a Jewish Yemenite named Miriam, the other a Jewish Iraqi girl (her name was Batya)—began writing letters (with the help of my father) to the then-Prime Minister, David Ben-Gurion (copies of which they sent to the daily newspapers), decrying the cruelty with which their husband was persecuted, while many Yemenite Jews, including rabbis (names enclosed) with three wives and four, went free. Finally, one day—this was in April, 1958, just before Passover—both wives (by then heavily pregnant) boarded the bus in Haifa and came to demonstrate before Ben Gurion's house in Tel Aviv, until, pregnant or not, BG's wife Paula came out and chased them away with a broomstick.

The rabbis in the Haifa Rabbinate didn't know what to do. First, because there was the matter of bad publicity, which no-one wants even in the best of times. But to make matters worse, this was when demands began to be made for civil marriage—in Israel one can marry only religiously—before a rabbi, a qadi, or a priest—so the last thing anyone wanted, was a proof that the rabbis permitted polygamy, because in comparison, civil marriage would seem reasonable.

But how to keep this quiet?

For a whole six months, diplomatic delegations were sent to Nathan, beseeching him to do as he was told, and quietly. Divorce any one of the wives he chose—it would then be ignored if he continued to live with both, so long as he was legally married to only one of them. Why, didn't Ben Gurion himself have his British mistress/secretary staying at his home, when she came to Israel to visit? Because his wife Paula preferred him sleeping with a woman she knew rather than with someone off the street?

Anyway, back to Nathan. First my father's cousins from Bney Barak, one of whom was head of a small yeshiva, went to see Nathan; then the other two, instructors in the Talmud sections of Divorces and Damages, went to see him, and all begged him, practically on bended knee, to give up, and not to make trouble. They even produced a special letter of entreaty written by R' Amatzia Sturman of Montreal, nicknamed the Second Luminescence and the greatest Adjudicator of the generation, alternately beseeching Nathan and adjuring him to make do with one wife, like the rest of the Jews. But nothing helped, and in the meantime Nathan's sons (Ury and Pinchas) were both born, so how could he even hear of a divorce?

But then the problem got even more complicated.

The complication happened when Nathan applied for the Childrens' Grant that the government had just instituted, and in the routine check-up on his Living Conditions, a social worker was sent from the Haifa regional welfare office to see the two children. And this worker—her name was Hadassah Tzigler, a good Ashkenazi girl from Haifa's poshest neighbourhood—fell in love with Nathan (no-one knows why), and began seeing him clandestinely; and from here to there, Nathan fell in love with her also, and after two months he up and proposed to her—which, after much trepidation (because, having been to his apartment in her professional capacity, she knew about the other two wives), she accepted.

By that time Nathan's case was famous, even though the newspapers didn't write about it (there was strong censorship those days), so no rabbi would marry him and Hadassah. Also, and just to be sure, the chief rabbi of the Haifa region (R' Zalman Shaposhnikov) issued an edict that any rabbi who dared marry Nathan Berkovitch again would be cut off from the referral list of weddings, circumcisions and burials. Which meant he would go to the poorhouse. So nu, after a month during which Nathan went even as far as the southern port city of Eilat, to get a rabbi for his third wedding, he gave up, and finally decided that, if he couldn't marry Hadassah legally, he would make her his pilegesh—his concubine. This way, if and when they had any children, the children at least would not be bastards—which they would be if Nathan, heaven forbid, had slept with a married woman, or had married the divorcée of a Cohen. Luckily, to take Hadassah as a pilegesh, all Nathan needed was her consent, which he had, and also the means to support her—which he had also, since his first wife had meantime begun to work too (in Dubek Cigarettes, on HaNavi Street).

So finally finally, in July 1958, against the hysterical objections of Hadassah's parents (both secular teachers in Haifa's Re'ali High School, and both good Laborites), Hadassah went to live with Nathan Berkovitch and his two wives and two children, in his apartment in Kiriat Bialik, and the very next year she bore him twin girls (Malka and Rachel), and that's when the story began to unravel.

What happened was, Nathan's first wife, Miriam (the Yemenite), had slipped in the bath and broke the tap. (Luckily nothing happened to her.) So she called a plumber, a man by the name of Jacob Shleif who worked with Nathan in the refineries and also did plumbing and sold Payis lottery tickets on the side, and after he had fixed the tap, he sold her a Payis lottery ticket and stayed for tea, and they began to talk. From here to there, she also saw him by chance in the Supersol grocery a few days later, and they talked some more—and nu, it developed. How exactly, no-one knows. But a month or so later, Miriam came to Nathan and told him she wanted Jacob to be her husband also, same as Nathan was.

At first Nathan refused. Not because of what you think— because he would have to share Miriam with another man; but because in the Bible, where there are lots of precedents of one man living with many women (the Patriarchs, Kings of Israel and Judea, and especially King Solomon), there are no precedents of one woman living with several men, unless one considers Jezebel, or Potiphar's wife, or other shady types. So at first Nathan objected. But then Miriam said that if that's the case, then all right, she'll divorce him and go live with Jacob, and Nathan immediately began to have second thoughts about his refusal. First, because he really loved Miriam. But second, and equally important, if he divorced Miriam, the Rabbinate's people would rejoice, and probably think they had managed to cow him. Yet my mother says that what really happened was, Nathan's other two wives—or rather, his other wife, Batya, and his pilegesh, Hadassah, went to him and said that what was good for him, should also be good for Miriam. Why should he be able to enjoy the favours of three women, when Miriam had to make do with one? So at last, after a month of negotiations in which my father, being Nathan's only brother, served as intermediary (Jacob Shleif, to his credit, did not stick his nose in), Nathan agreed to Miriam's request, and merely put forward one condition: that they all move to a larger apartment, since the three-room flat they were then occupying in Kiryat Bialik, was bursting already—what with him, Nathan, and three women, and four children. It was so tight, that children had to take turns sleeping in one bed, and women took turns sleeping in Nathan's bed. Once I heard my father whisper to my mother that he would not be surprised to learn that every now and then more than one woman slept in Nathan's bed, with Nathan. But my mother said no-one knows this for sure, and not to sin with his mouth. So who knows.

But to cut to the main point: in January 1961, Nathan sold his apartment in Kiryat Bialik, and he and his two wives (Miriam and Batya) and his pilegesh (Hadassah) and their four children (Ury and Pinchas, and Malka and Rachel) moved into a five-room flat in upper Haifa (on HaBonim Street, #13) together with Jacob Shleif, the plumber. Jacob and Miriam lived in one room, and Nathan in another. The other wife, Batya, and the pilegesh, Hadassah, as far as I know slept together in one room, and the kids shared the other two: the three boys in one room (Miriam in the meantime gave birth to another son, named Immanuel, from Jacob), the girls in the other. Whether Miriam still shared Nathan's bed from time to time, I don't know; also whether Hadassah or Batya ever visited Jacob Shleif. Nobody ever talked about this in the family. But as far as my father could see (he went to visit several times), they were all happy there, until April 1963, when Miriam won 150,000 *Lirot* in the Payis lottery.

In those days, 150,000 *Lirot* was real money, something like maybe a million today. So the winning immediately threw the happy Berkovitch-Shleif household into deep schisms. Because even though everyone seemed happy and content before, as in every other family there were always little problems that could be blown up with the proper amount of bad luck. And 150,000 *Lirot* was a truly big piece of bad luck, especially when it came out that Miriam's winning Payis ticket had been bought with five *Lirot* she had borrowed from Hadassah. Or rather Miriam insisted she had borrowed the money—the five *Lirot* bill was lying on the kitchen table (Miriam said), and when she saw it, she asked Hadassah in a clear voice whether she (Miriam) could borrow it; and Hadassah (this Miriam remembered most distinctly) said Yes. So (said Miriam), all she now owed Hadassah—whom she loved like a sister—was the five *Lirot*, and nothing else. And to corroborate her claim, she brought forth the testimony of Batya, who had just come into the kitchen to fry an egg, and so heard Miriam utter the words, "Can I borrow the five *Lirot* from you?"

Unfortunately, Batya said in her testimony that all she had heard was, "Can I borrow five *Lirot*?" without "the" and without "from you," and, moreover, she did not hear at all Hadassah's answer, if indeed there had been one.

So this started the ball rolling, with Hadassah insisting she had not loaned the five *Lirot* to Miriam, and hinting that Miriam had taken it without permission, so that even a beginning rabbi could see immediately that anything bought with this money-taken-without-permission was hers, and hers alone. Same as the original money was hers, Hadassah's, to share with whomever she wished—which happened to be her two girls (Malka and Rachel).

Nu, you can imagine how it developed. Before long there was shouting and screaming, accusations and counter-accusations and digging up of ancient quarrels, and also, shame to admit, tearing of hair, and even fisticuffs. By that time, the dispute began to involve not just the immediate Berkovitch-Shleif family (Nathan,

Jacob, Miriam, Batya, Hadassah, and the five children), but also my father, who was brought in as an honest mediator, and then my mother, who was brought in to explain to my father some of the women's words which at first seemed to mean not what he thought they meant, but just the opposite. So maybe two days a week, my father would close his shoe-store in Tel Aviv, and take the train to Haifa and return in the evening, looking haggard. And did he need this problem? Like a hole in the head he needed it. But what could he do? Nothing. He had to help his brother because all the other brothers (in Poland) went with Hitler—and also to keep it quiet, because who wants such family mish-mash to go out? No-one. At least (and this was the only blessing), the mish-mash was still being kept inside the Berkovitch family, because Jacob Shleif, to his credit, still did not bring anyone of his own into it.

And it all might have stayed this way, if not for one small detail. It then came out that the five *Lirot* that Hadassah had said were hers, were not really hers at all, but rather belonged to Batya's son Ury. It was the gift-money he had received in the Passover Seder the month before from Nathan, and he, Ury, then loaned it to his Aunt Hadassah (that's what the children called each other's mothers) so that she could buy Nathan a present for his birthday. And although none of this was in dispute—neither Batya nor Hadassah denied that the boy had loaned Hadassah the five *Lirot*—did this mean that the winning Payis ticket was really Hadassah's? Just because a boy too-young-to-be-a-witness (by the Talmud) had loaned the money to her? And even if this was so, did Hadassah now owe some of the winning to Batya's boy? And if she admitted even this, didn't she imply by this admission that Miriam also had rights in the money which she, Miriam, claimed to have borrowed from Hadassah?

To add to this mish-mash, Nathan, to whom the winning ticket had been entrusted for safekeeping, refused to give it back to either Hadassah or Miriam. First, on the grounds that he did not know who was right, and showing favour to either disputant would cast him in the role of a Dishonest Judge, preferring one side to the other, where he himself had a clear connection to both. But second and worse, he would thereby also become an Immoral Husband, by showing preference to one wife over the other. (The Talmud sages, like the Biblical Patriarchs, of course had several wives each.) So Nathan said he would give the winning ticket to neither one, until matters were settled.

This raised the dispute to ever higher levels, involving progressively more members of the Berkovitch-Shleif family. At first Nathan's Bney Barak cousins came to give advice; then Jacob Shleif, for the first time, began to express his opinion too. (He was in favour of dividing the money equally, or at least equitably, although he was a bit vague about who should be included in the first case, or what would be meant by the second.) Finally, Hadassah's parents waded in also, each offering advice, and girl-friends of Hadassah from the Haifa welfare office, each weighing in with a different opinion altogether. As a result of all this, my father's absences from his shoe-store lengthened to three days a week, and when he now left to arbitrate the ballooning dispute, he often took with him a Tel Aviv senior family court rabbi as an advisor in Jewish religious law. Once or twice my mother went along also (in which case I had to skip school and stay in the store); but nothing helped. The dispute only mushroomed ever larger, until it finally blew up when Batya claimed that Hadassah's and Miriam's claims notwithstanding, she, as Ury's mother, had natural rights in her boy's money, and acting as a Parental Fiduciary she could sue on his behalf before a Rabbinical Court—indeed, she had a moral obligation to do so, to protect his interest. And that's exactly what she finally did.

Two months after the Payis lottery win, when the mish-mash was already good and ripe, Batya Berkovitch climbed on bus No. 301 from Haifa to Tel Aviv, disembarked on Allenby Street, and went straight to the Rabbinate's main hall, where, to the consternation of the old clerk (the father of Haifa's chief Rabbi), she lodged a formal Torah Suit against her Tzara—which is the derogatory Biblical term for The Other Wife—claiming Theft and Usurpation and Undue Coercion (via forcing a minor to testify against his natural mother), and several other complaints besides. And if that was not bad enough, Batya really threw the shmaltz into the fire when, the next day, she hired Getzl Goldman, my mother's crazy brother, (who has been studying unsuccessfully to be a rabbi for the past twelve years), as her rabbinical advocate, to plead her case before the Tel Aviv Rabbinical Court (Northern Circuit)—the very same court that had been trying for the past five years on behalf of the Haifa Rabbinate, without success, to force Nathan to divorce her.

Now let me make a little pause here. Because this Getzl, let me tell you, his name in the Rabbinate was mud. First, because he had never been formally ordained as a rabbi; and even though there is no rule that every rabbinical advocate must be a rabbi, that's usually the case. But second and worse was, that after twelve years of wildly ranging and unfocused study, Getzl knew so many obscure and useless annotations to the Bible and the Talmud and the Mishna, that, if he so wanted, he could show off most other rabbinical advocates as ignoramuses by raising useless objections based on past precedents no-one had ever heard of. This wasted everyone's time, having to go look for the citations (since Getzl was not beyond inventing imaginary sources), then refute them with other sources, a low trick that no true rabbinical advocate would employ, because then it could be done to him too.

But third and trickiest, Getzel only made his advocacy in Yiddish.

Now why was this so insidious? Because, in those days, there was the beginning of the coalition agreement that would in future provide to all yeshiva students no matter what age, free lodging and room and board (and a little stipend) and also exempt them from the army, so long as they studied the Torah. This was a very tantalizing prospect for yeshiva heads (most of whom augmented their meagre income with rabbinical advocacy), since the coalition agreement would flow more money to yeshivas, and so add to their income a little—let alone the further augmentation that could result from the power to exempt yeshiva students from the draft. So naturally these heady prospects made rabbinical advocates very cautious about how they appeared before the civil authorities; and the first step they undertook was to hold all Rabbinical Court sessions in Hebrew, rather than in Yiddish. This sudden Hebrew speaking was a bit hard on some old rabbis who spoke Yiddish only, and in dialect, while Hebrew prayers they knew only by rote—same as they knew the Bible. But with a view for the future good of the community, they all made the effort and adapted.

All, that is, except a hardcore conservative few, chief among them Getzel Goldman, who (begging your pardon) like old Catholic priests sticking to Latin mass, insisted on speaking Yiddish in rabbinical court also. So when Batya hired Getzl as her rabbinical advocate, it was clear to everyone she was ratcheting up the stakes by a threat that, if she didn't win her case, she was going to make trouble for everyone, cost what may.

The other wife and the pilegesh, Miriam and Hadassah, at first appeared in propria persona, representing themselves; but then, on the prospects of their share in the Payis winnings, they each got herself a famous rabbininal advocate: Hadassah hired the New York Boyberishe Rebbe's son-in-law (—and was *he* ever expensive!); and Miriam hired a Yemenite rabbinical advocate (who later became Israel's Chief Sephardic Rabbi). And these two, plus Getzl Goldman, soon flooded the Tel Aviv Rabbinate with so many indignant letters and submissions and counter-submissions and responses and objections and counter-objections, that two new clerks had to be hired, and then also a third, and of course also a Yiddish-Hebrew translator.

Now, you should remember that right about that time (May, 1963), the Tel Aviv Rabbinate had just merged with the Yaffo Rabbinate, and so had become the most powerful rabbinical court in Israel—more powerful than the Jerusalem Rabbinate, even. Naturally there was a lot of resentment against this powerful new court by rabbis everywhere, but especially in Haifa, which was then a "red" workers' town controlled by a wily Laborite apparatchik. Because of their "red" milieu, the Haifa rabbis were always an object of pity and condescension—to which sentiments my Uncle Nathan's double-marriage only added. So at first, the mish-mash with the Payis ticket of the Berkovitch-Shleif household just increased the mirth in the Tel Aviv-Jaffa Rabbinate at the expense of the Haifa rabbis; which of course only augmented the Haifa rabbis' resentment. For a while this discord threatened to add to the conflagration, as Tel Aviv Torah briefs went unanswered and Haifa rabbinical requests were quietly disparaged. So much so, that the chief Israeli rabbi tried to mediate the dispute, but without success. Even adjurements (through letters) by the great R' Sturman of Montreal were to no avail. But when the case blossomed into what it finally became, both mirth and resentment subsided fast, and the need for mediation evaporated, as the entire rabbinical establishment united in defence against the potential religious-legal disaster.

And why disaster? Because right about then, there happened the first of those chance occurrences that turned the "Payis Case" (as it later became known) into the biggest and most complicated religious-law dispute in the history of the Israeli rabbinical courts. So big and complicated, that learned rabbis began arriving—at their own expense—from as far away as Buenos Aires and Caracas and Gstaad, to give their opinions—for free—about the Torah solution to all this mish-mash, so as to save Jewish Religious Law from itself. Only at the end, when Rabbi Amatzia Sturman of Montreal, the Second Luminescence himself, arrived and stood in the breech, did the danger pass. But until that moment, there existed the possibility that the Gershomite dictum against polygamy would be overturned, and with it, all of R' Gershomm's other rulings—and with them, the rulings of all Adjudicators who came after—and so all Torah rulings of the last 1000 years would be undone. And then where would all Jews be?

But let me not jump too far ahead like a goat, and tell everything in order. Because right then happened the first bombshell.

What happened was, in the middle of the second mediating session, Nathan suddenly announced that none of the children was his.

Can you imagine?

When the uproar subsided, Nathan said that since the children-who-were-not-his were all born while their mothers were married to him, they were all bastards according to the Torah, and so could not inherit anything—either from their mothers or from him—because bastards had no right to receive property from any Jewish person. (Talmud Bavli, Purity Section, chapter Gimmel.) So even if the children had acquired any property by chance, their mother(s) had no fiduciary part and/or obligation(s) in this regard either. And since in any case the money in question was originally given by Nathan to Ury, it was still Nathan's. So anything done with it and any fruit it bore from any use it was put to whatsoever, was legally Nathan's and his alone.

And even if—just suppose!—even if someone had tried to cast doubt about the origin of these five *Lirot*, any money lying on a table in the house was in the category of Found Money, as defined in the Talmud, and thus belonged to the Man of the House—namely Nathan Berkovitch—upon production of a valid title-deed to the apartment—which he had—and a marriage certificate—which he had also (two of them). So the five *Lirot* were entirely his, Nathan said, on at least two counts: the first actual and the second theoretical (though not less strong) and so the lottery ticket and the winnings thereof were his too, Q.E.D. And what other proof would anyone else with a head on his shoulders require? Huh? Huh?

Yet the above bombshell, as you surely know (if you read the papers), was of course not the end of it. Because in the meantime, although the Rabbinical Court filings are supposed to be secret, word had somehow leaked out to the lottery management, and the Payis directors realized that this could become a very hot mish-mash indeed. So right away they got themselves a civil court injunction, locking up the disputed funds in an interest-bearing escrow account in Bank Leumi, until ownership of the lottery ticket was clarified, either in a civil court by a judge, or by a ruling of a qualified rabbi in a Rabbinical Court, or by a fatwa of a qadi in a Shari'a Court, or via a government Order-in-Council—

none of whom would of course touch the matter with a long broomstick.

In short, it was a real hot mish-mash as if designed by the Heavens to make trouble for poor rabbis.

And perhaps this was indeed the case? Who can say no? Maybe God indeed does do such things from time to time, to tell the Jews what they otherwise don't want to hear? Because even though there could still have been an amicable solution to all this, the second bombshell then exploded as if on cue. In the next joint-appearance of Nathan and his wives and pilegesh in the forced-mediation hearing, Nathan stated to the chief adjudicating rabbi, R' Shaposhnikov, that not only Nathan's children were bastards, but that his wives had other men on the side, too; and so they were whores.

When Nathan said this word, all mediation was of course out of the question. And not only that, but when Batya heard Nathan say this word, she hit him on the head with her shoe's heel, and when he tried to hit her in return, Hadassah grabbed his hand and tried to hit him too (on the face); and then Miriam also hit him (on the chin), and tried to scratch his eyes. And when Nathan tried to defend himself, he pushed them off and both wives fell down. So Getzl Goldman, Batya's rabbinical advocate, intervened and pushed Nathan back and also slapped him twice on the face, the first on his client's behalf and the second on his own. And when R' Shaposhnikov's father (the court's clerk) tried to get in between to make peace, he was slapped by everybody. So his son (the Court's chief rabbi) ran down from the bench to defend his father—because the duty of a son to his father (as appears in the Ten Commandments) precedes the duty of a judge to his litigants. But it is also possible that R' Shaposhnikov remembered how

Nathan had made laughing stock of the entire Haifa Rabbinate for five years, which is why he kicked Nathan five times. (My father says seven, but who knows.)

Be that as it may, in the big mish-mash that ensued, the police, shameful to admit, had to be called, and all brawlers, litigants and advocates were dragged out of the courtroom and driven in black police cruisers to the Abu Kabbir jail in Jaffa. And it is only because my father knew one of the jail guards (whose father was also from Radom, the Polish town my father came from), that they were all let out in the morning without having to go see another judge, and without bail, just on their own word and promise. (Also, my father later said, because of the coalition agreement. But who knows.)

What is sure, though, is that from that moment on, the mish-mash spun out of control. That very same morning Nathan asked Miriam to leave the apartment and to take Jacob with her. But— listen to this: she said No! Especially after what Nathan had said about his wives having men on the side—did anyone ever hear of such a thing? She had every right to stay and clear her name (she said), and also get what was due her: her share in the Payis lottery ticket, and her share in the apartment, and also a big apology.

Jacob, to his credit, still did not mix in it, and just said he would stick by Miriam no matter what. Nathan thought at first to throw Jacob out too, but because Jacob was a plumber and worked with his hands, and Nathan was only a bookkeeper and not too strong, what could he do? Nothing. So Jacob stayed; and when Nathan tried to order Hadassah and Batya to leave, they also said they were staying, to look after their property and their children, and, like Miriam, to defend their honour and good name. And if

Nathan didn't retract his slander, there would be another Torah Suit, they said, only this time for libel and evil tongue. And how would he like that? Huh? Huh?

That very day in court, both Miriam and Batya said they wanted the suit for slander to proceed in parallel with the Payis Ticket Case, and insisted on filing the papers that very noon. At the mention of yet one more Torah Suit, R' Shaposhnikov (who after a night in the Abu Kabbir jail, was completely sick of both Tel Aviv and the litigants and only wanted to go back to his family in Haifa), shouted that there would be no further lawsuits. And when the women (or rather their advocates) insisted, R' Shaposhnikov screamed at Nathan, and ordered him to retract his allegations immediately or at least say he hadn't meant what he had said! But Nathan, obstinate like a mule, refused to retract anything—not a single word. He insisted everything he had said was true—true like the sun at mid-day and the moon at night—so he would retract nothing. If his two wives wanted to sue him, let them. He would prove everything he had said.

R' Shaposhnikov threatened Nathan with jail (which rabbinical courts can do) if he didn't recant, but after a night in Abu Kabbir, was this such a big scare for him? No. So Nathan kept refusing to apologize and again offered to prove his words were true. And when the judge hollered at him that proof of that nature was very hard to present in a rabbinical court, Nathan asked for a delay of a day so he could get his own rabbinical advocate to help.

R' Shaposhnikov nearly broke down, but had to agree. After all, how can you prevent a Jew from getting proper Scriptural advice?

And so the court adjourned, and next day Nathan returned with a rabbinical advocate who was the grandson of a great Safed kabbalist, and this advocate, the very first time he opened his mouth, dropped the third and biggest bombshell of all.

Before the dense crowd of shocked lay people and rabbis (many from as far away as Berlin and Geneva), Nathan's advocate said that Nathan was (tfu tfu tfu) sterile. His seeds were so mish-mashed, that they couldn't swim. So even though Nathan could still favour women (else why would they marry him?) he was completely unable to beget children.

When this came out (my father said), you could have heard a skullcap drop in the courtroom. And when Nathan's advocate, with a modest flourish, produced a certificate from Dr. Rivkin (from Rambam Hospital) proving this both in Hebrew and in Yiddish, and with his signature and two government stamps too, there was a collective gasp and a shudder in the court. Because, can you imagine? A man with two wives and a pilegesh—and sterile?

But after the shock subsided, came the obvious question: so whose were the four children?

R' Shaposhnikov (the court chairman) began to question Nathan, not gently, and little by little out came this: first off, Nathan said he had told both his wives at the beginning about his affliction, and he had told his pilegesh as well.

So (asked R' Shaposhnikov), why did they agree to marry you, and Hadassah to come live with you?

Maybe, Nathan said, because I was otherwise all right (on which adjective he refused to elaborate), and also because I had a good job. But because every family needs children, to fulfill God's command to multiply, we all decided we'd get good seed from someone else—a friend maybe, or a volunteer—and mix this seed with mine, and use this mish-mash with a syringe, like with (begging your Honour's pardon) cows in a kibbutz. And who knows?

Maybe God will smile upon us?

And that's exactly what happened, Nathan continued (after the gasping died down). When the wives got the seed from the volunteer and mixed it with Nathan's, by a miracle it worked, and God did indeed smile upon the two wives and upon the pilegesh, and they all got pregnant immediately. So this was why the children were all bastards, Nathan said, and the lottery ticket belonged to him alone.

Nu, you can imagine?! When finally came out all this, in more detail than I wrote here, the courtroom in the Rabbinate became like the Carmel market, everyone shouted together, and two elderly rabbis from Bney Barak fainted and had to be taken to Beilnsohn hospital. (But after they got Valerian to smell in the ambulance they made the driver stop driving, and straightaway ran back to court to hear the rest.)

Then of course happened the inevitable: With this last revelation, no detail of the case could be kept out of the papers any longer. First, *HaOlam HaZe*, Israel's first yellow rag, published a cover story about the "Ashkenazi Yemenite" from Haifa and his many wives (they made it four wives, and not just one pilegesh but two), and his winning ticket (they made Nathan the winner, and in the soccer pool, not the Payis lottery, and of a quarter million *Lirot*; but the other parts they got correct). And a day after *HaOlam HaZe* came out, *Ha'Aretz* (which is like the *New York Times*, only even more Liberal) also printed the story, but in a restrained manner; and finally finally also came *HaTzofeh*, the paper of the religious party, which wrote a long article about the entire mishmash. (They were also the first ones who called it by this name.) And this article got *HaTzofeh*'s editor fired (because of all the enraged letters the publishers got from rabbis' wives), and so his

assistant got his job. And then the fired editor got himself a civil
lawyer and sued *HaTozfeh*'s publishers (which at the time was the
Rabbinate itself) in civil court—can you believe this imperti-
nence?—because who has ever heard of one religious Jew suing
another before the secular authorities? It's a scandal! Who is above
whom here?! And all of this because of what? Because of a Payis
ticket and two wives and a pilegesh and a second husband?

Yet two days later, as the trial against the Rabbinate (launched by
the fired *HaTzofeh*'s editor) was gearing up, there happened
worse: When the Rabbinical Court's clerk asked Nathan, for the
record, who were the friends whose seed he had mixed with his
to beget his bastard children, Nathan's two wives and Hadassah
sprang up and began to scream and yell, adjuring Nathan to keep
quiet. But some yeshiva boys in the crowd helped the court-guards
to restrain the women, and so Nathan could speak. And when he
finally spoke, he said that (as you may have suspected) the volunteer had been none other than Jacob.

This was no longer such a big shock. The shock was what came
after, which was this: Jacob Shleif, who did plumbing for the
refineries and also sold Payis lottery tickets (and pencils and New
Year greeting cards too), also made money on the side donating
his seed to the Seed-Bank in Rambam Hospital, where Dr. Rivkin
(the brother of the famous cancer doctor) was treating infertile
poor Jews to help them multiply. And Nathan, who had known
about this because he worked with Jacob in the refineries and
also had fought alongside him in the War of Independence, in '48,
asked Jacob if he would mind if Nathan took this seed for his
wives—because it was better to get seed from someone you knew
was healthy, and also not an Arab, than from a stranger. The

problem was, normally if you went through Rambam hospital to get seed, the donor remained anonymous, because Dr. Rivkin was in the middle like a veil. But if you asked for someone you knew, then maybe he would feel badly when you met him later in the street, or at work? But Jacob said he didn't care, and Nathan said, if you don't, I don't either. So that's what happened. Nathan asked Dr. Rivkin to give Jacob's seeds to his wives, and that's how Nathan's first four children were born.

But after a while, Nathan began to think about it, and he said to Jacob, Why do we have to go through Rambam? I can pay you directly—more than what you would get if we went through the Hospital and Dr. Rivkin took his cut, but less than what I would pay Dr. Rivkin.

Nu, because Payis tickets and pencils didn't exactly sell too well that year, Jacob said all right, how much will you pay? Nathan mentioned a price, but Jacob said he wanted more, and they could not agree. So finally Nathan said, Come to the house tomorrow, we'll talk about it. But to prevent the evil tongues from wagging in case something became known, when Jacob arrived next day it was as-if-to-fix the tap that Miriam as-if-broke. This was the plan. But what wasn't in the plan, was that when Miriam saw Jacob (she never saw him before, only his seed), she fell in love with him, which nobody could foretell (only God can). So what can you do? Nothing.

Now when came out all this, four more rabbis fainted (all from Haifa), and R' Shaposhnikov, who was just about to announce a recess, nearly fainted too. But just as the fainted rabbis were being carried out on litters (R' Shaposhnikov refused to be moved), Miriam jumped to her feet, pushed her advocate aside, and, waving her arms in the air, shouted that all right, since Nathan told this part, she'll tell the rest. All of it!

From surprise, one of the carriers dropped his litter (the rabbi who fell later sued him), and the three other carriers stopped so the fainted rabbis could listen. And lucky for them, because Miriam's next words threw the case into the very high orbit that threatened to wreck more than ten centuries of Jewish Torah law.

According to Miriam, the truth was this: when Jacob came in, he first drank tea (which she made for him), and was very polite to her. Then she left the kitchen, and Jacob and Nathan immediately began to haggle, because what Nathan offered was still too cheap, and what Jacob wanted was still too high. Only after an hour Jacob finally came down to 40 *Lirot* for his seed (he had begun at 80), and Nathan came up to 30 (he had begun with ten).

Here R' Shaposhnikov had to quiet the courtroom repeatedly, and issue several threats to the rabbis' wives who clicked their tongues ever more loudly each time a new detail came out. When silence was finally established, R' Shaposhnikov asked Miriam how she knew all these details. How? she said. How could she not? Nathan and Jacob argued loudly in the kitchen while she was in the nearby bedroom darning children's socks (the children were in school). So she heard the entire thing to the end, when Nathan and Jacob were only five *Lirot* apart—Nathan said 35, and Jacob still said 40. But then Nathan broke the deadlock by saying, All right, 35, and you can contribute your seed to Miriam any way you want. Jacob said he was agreeable—but only so long as Miriam agreed too.

At this point the court had to be recessed for an hour and some screaming spectators cleared out, including two reporters. And when the court reconvened, Miriam went on and testified that when she overheard this, she decided immediately to agree—not because she wanted to sin with Jacob (whom she'd just met), but to take revenge on Nathan who had valued her honour at five *Lirot* only.

When came out all this tall-tale, R' Shaposhnikov was so over-come, that he had to be taken out on a litter, and one of the four other adjudicating rabbis, R' Simcha Sturman, had to take over. This R' Simcha was a grand nephew of R' Amatzia Sturman from Montreal, the Second Luminescence, the very man who saved all Jewish Religious Law a week later. But let me not jump ahead, because right after R' Shaposhnikov was taken to hospital, came out the last bombshell (by Miriam), which was this: when Nathan paid Jacob his money, he gave Jacob four bills of ten *Lirot* each, since he did not have anything smaller. But because Jacob did not have change either, how do you think he gave Nathan change?

If you said with a Payis lottery ticket worth five *Lirot*, you are exactly right.

When finally came out this last part—and as it became clear that the entire story about the borrowed five *Lirot* had been a tall-tale, to save the honour of the Berkovitch-Shleif family—the ballooning legal mish-mash showed the first signs of what it was finally to become: a Kushiyat Tophet (a Hell-Problem). This is the Talmudic term for a hypothetical question composed by the Devil himself, that cannot be solved by the Torah's Laws, no matter how much the smartest rabbis might try. And why is such a Kushiya so dangerous? Because one of the Torah's corner-stones is the saying (by rabbi Tarfon): "Turn it and turn it, and everything is in it,"—meaning that every problem can be solved by the Halacha—the accumulation of Jewish Torah Laws—so a Jew needs no other laws to live his life. The direct implication is that if even one Jewish problem could not be solved by the Halachah, the entire edifice of Jewish Law would tumble down, as the failure proved that Jews also needed other laws to live by, besides the Laws of God.

And if this were the case (tfu tfu tfu!), were would Jews be? In a dark legal mish-mash, that's where, with both God and the Other One contending for Jewish souls daily, each claiming His law was better than the other's in this one case.

Can you imagine?

Small wonder then, that the subject of Hell-Problem is one that only very few scholars are allowed to study—and even so, only after the age of 40. Just like the Matter of the Chariot—the flaming chair carrying the divinity that the prophet Ezekiel saw on the bank of the river Kvar in Babylon—and just as the study of the Kabbalah and numerical Combinations is restricted. All because—in theory—these subjects have the potential of ruining a Jew's faith by falsely proving to him the existence of rules besides Jewish law that are necessary to sustain life.

But since some readers of this tale may be too tender-minded to contemplate such lofty matters, or maybe too young, let's say no more of this and go back to the story, where, more and more, it now became apparent to everyone that what had begun simply with a Payis lottery ticket, a man with two wives, one pilegesh and a co-husband, has developed into that legendary rabbinical nightmare—a Hell-Problem that might not be soluble by the Jewish Halacha alone.

Matters began to deteriorate rapidly soon thereafter, when Jacob Shleif also got himself a rabbinical advocate (from Be'er Sheva), and this one now claimed that, Miriam's testimony notwithstanding, his client (Jacob) had not handed the ticket directly to Nathan. Rather, when Jacob had finished giving his contribution to Miriam (in a jar), he left the ticket on her bedside table (under the jar). And it was this ticket, not the one that Batya said she had bought with the five *Lirot*, that won the lottery.

So theoretically, since the ticket was given to Miriam, it could be construed as Etnan-Zonah, payment-to-a-loose-woman for services rendered, and so belonged to Miriam, not to Nathan or anyone else.

Pandemonium would be too weak a word to describe what took place in the courtroom after this revelation—which was conveyed directly to the government that same afternoon. Because by that time, several government observers were already coming every day to see how the matter was developing, as the trial and all the noise surrounding it were slowing down the coalition negotiations with the religious parties. For how can any responsible official negotiate for yeshiva funds, when no-one even knew whether what was taught in yeshivas would still be valid tomorrow? Perhaps no post-Bible religious rulings could hold up before the hellish theoretical onslaught now taking place on Allenby Street? Maybe tomorrow's yeshiva boys could not even study the Talmud, or the Mishna? Perhaps they could study only the book of Genesis and nothing else? Or maybe only Genesis' first chapter? What then of all the crucial chapters in Exodus, Numbers or Deuteronomy, where God promised the land of Canaan to his chosen people? What then?

This, and more, came up in furtive whispers between spectators in recess, and in mutters over tea glasses in the court's kosher cafeteria, where pale rabbis stuttered hoarsely about the danger to the last 1000 years of Jewish Law—perhaps to the very patrimony!

Matters became so tense, it was said, that the Prime Minister himself (Ben Gurion) was receiving daily briefings about the trial from the chief Israeli rabbi, whose beadle attended every court session and took notes.

Not that he needed to—there was so much written about the trial in both newspapers and magazines (though the radio of course said nothing), that the Prime Minister could have read it all by buying a newspaper. Matter of fact, the entire country was talking about little else besides the Lottery Ticket Given as Whore's Payment by the Man who Came to Favour the Wife of the Sterile Man with Two Wives and a Pilegesh. Even the secular newspapers dedicated whole sections over the weekend to readers' suggestions on solving the insoluble Kushiya of deciding who the winning lottery ticket belonged to. Because underlying all the frivolity, was the very real dread that, if this case could not be resolved by the Jewish Hallacha, then all Jewish Torah Law of the last 1000 years would be in trouble—perhaps even all Jewish Religious Law from the days of the Babylon Exile. And where would the Jews be then? Huh? Huh?

It was then that the matter was brought to the attention of R' Amatzia Sturman of Montreal, the Second Luminescence himself (who already knew about Nathan Berkovitch from the time he had been asked to adjure him to divorce one of his wives, without success). And why was the question brought to R' Amatzia's attention? Because R' Shaposhnikov (the court's chief) was still in hospital, and so the alternate head adjudicator was R' Simcha Sturman, the S.L.'s grand nephew. And was this not another proof of divine intervention?

Be that as it may, R' Simcha now prevailed upon the other adjudicators to write to his famous great-uncle and ask for his help. And so, a month after the Payis trial began, the Tel Aviv-Jaffa rabbinical court sent the S.L. an urgent telegram, both in Hebrew and in Yiddish, formally asking for immediate guidance.

Although the Second Luminescence had just turned 91, and his prostate had grown as large as an orange from the evils of Canadian weather, he could recognize in the telegram's entreaty the finger of God pointing to him a duty he must perform. And can anyone refuse such a direct order? No. So in the depth of the Montreal winter, R' Amatzia Sturman packed his phylacteries bag, stuffed spare large underwear into his satchel, and with the financial help of the congregation's wealthier members (the Bronsky family) bought an Air Canada ticket to New York; and from there, an El Al ticket to Tel Aviv.

He arrived at Lodd airport on 2 February, 1964 in the afternoon, and with the last of his Canadian dollars hired a cab and told the driver to drive straight to the rabbinical courtroom on Allenby Street in Tel Aviv.

When Rabbi Amatzia Sturman limped into the Allenby courtroom with his legs spread, nine rabbis, including five famous Safed kabbalists, rose from their chairs and prostrated themselves. His grand-nephew of course rushed to his famed great uncle's side, both to help him walk, and to be perfumed by his status, then offered him a seat by his own side, at the dais.

But R' Amatzia waved all admirers away, pulled a pillow from his travel bag, plopped it on a bench in the last row, and sat down carefully. Then, dismissing his grand-nephew back to the judges' table, he signalled to him with a wiggle of his spidery fingers to please continue and not to mind him. He was just a spectator in this court, he said; just as the Blessed Holy Name surely was.

At the mention of special providential attention to the proceedings, the spectators rustled with elation and panic, and a few rabbis' wives took out their Tzena u'Renas—the Yiddish translation of the Pentateuch. Even seasoned rabbis in the audience pulled out small Psalms books, to be on the safe side. For did not people say that at a word from the Second Luminescence's mouth, the angels themselves cocked an ear? Wasn't he the one-in-a-generation rabbi whose reasoned arguments in favour of studying the Matter of the Chariot (Ezekiel, chapter 1) were declared both valid and too dangerous to pursue? Was he not the one and only rabbi who, in the eventful year 1952, had dared decree that a bastard in the seventh generation could escape his stigma, and marry like any other Jew, by converting to Judaism as if he were a complete gentile?

This same juridicial daredevil now sat on his pillow at the back row, bearded chin in cupped hand, listening to my maternal uncle Getzel reason out loud why my paternal uncle Nathan Berkovitch should give up the Payis ticket—which was not a Whore's Payment as claimed by the other litigants, but rather a Thing Given unto Safekeeping by a wife who had entrusted her husband with a keepsake.

Getzel was well into his argument when R' Amatzia raised a thin forefinger and asked in Yiddish whether he could ask the plaintiff a question—just a little one.

Getzel's flow of words stopped in mid-vowel. The entire courtroom fell silent as everyone in the room turned back, and the spectators sitting in the front got up to stare backwards. My father said it was as if all adjudicators had suddenly emigrated to the back row, and everyone had to turn around for the trial to proceed. But the Second Luminescence did not seem to notice. He just stared mildly at my Uncle Getzel through wide blue eyes, and Getzl became all flustered and answered (in Yiddish) that of course the Second Luminescence could ask any question he wanted—he, Getzel would be happy to answer—

At which point the S.L. wagged his thin finger and said in

broken Hebrew that he wanted to ask a question not of him, but of the plaintiff.

Getzel nodded shakily and sat down.

There was absolute silence in the courtroom, as everyone waited without moving a hair, as they say, until finally R' Amatzia asked Miriam in a very mild voice whether he could take a look at the lottery ticket in question.

Flustered, she said she did not have the lottery ticket—Nathan had it.

The S.L. turned to Nathan, who, to everyone's surprise, pulled a small envelope out of his shirt pocket and, walking slowly to the back row (perhaps to show he was not awed by any rabbinical eminence), gave the envelope into R' Amatzia's hand.

The crowd held its breath as the S.L. pulled out the checkered black and white square of paper, and held it up to the light in his emaciated fingers.

This? the S.L. asked in a mild voice. This is the object of contention?

My father said he felt like a cold fingernail on his spine, seeing this little paper that was threatening to sink ten centuries of Jewish Law. It was as if the presence of a Higher Being had entered the courtroom. But whether it was the presence of God, or of his Opponent—or maybe both—who could say?

All spectators and adjudicators gaped at the ticket, including the litigants.

Is this the object? The S.L. repeated.

Jacob Shleif said diffidently, What is the number, please?

R' Amatzia pulled a pair of narrow reading glasses from his frayed jacket and read out the number, first in Yiddish, then in Hebrew.

Jacob nodded, then Batya, and Miriam; finally Nathan gave a curt nod also. Yes, this was the ticket in question. The very same.

The air in the court became charged with electricity like Ezekiel's chariot, as the S.L. scrutinized the little ticket. But electricity turned into thrilled shudders as the old eminence raised his eyes and said that the answer to the Kushiya was very simple. In fact, he could not see why everyone had made such a mish-mash of it.

There was absolute silence in the courtroom as R' Amatzia went on and said that, not only was the answer simple, but it was in the original Torah, not the latter Talmud or Mishna. Why, could no-one present recall the relevant guidance given in very similar circumstances by that most famous of Biblical kings, who was wise in all things except in the matter of wives?

Feverish whispers flew through the audience. What answer to this Kushiya in the Torah was so obvious that the best Jewish minds of the generation had missed it?

A few rabbis took out notebooks; reporters activated their tape-recorders; and two rabbis' wives had pulled out lorgnettes—when a deep-throated gasp rose in the courtroom. Because R' Amatzia Sturman, the Second Luminescence, greatest Jewish adjudicator since Rabbi Gershom himself, pulled a pair of scissors out of his pocket, and put them to the winning lottery ticket.

All litigants began to shout at once. The four adjudicators cried out in alarm. The court's clerks, gasping, rose to their feet. Nathan jumped to his feet also.

Yes! Cut it! Nathan shouted. Cut! Neither I nor they will have it, but at least we'll live in peace, like before!

No! shouted Miryam. No! Don't cut! Give it to the children!

Batya and Hadassah, too, called to let the children have the winnings.

Yes, Jacob said simply. Yes.

It was, my father says, as if a great wind had blown through the courtroom. One moment panic, the second, elation. If before there had been sheer pandemonium, now there were joyous shouts, and heartfelt cries, and finally a few handclaps that grew in volume until they turned into a feet-stomping applause. So much so, that two constables from police headquarters at Harakevett Street, more than half a kilometre away, soon burst in with their Parabelums drawn, a moment after the judgment had been given, to see what disaster had taken place.

But disaster, of course, had been averted, because judgment was handed down unanimously even before the applause died down. The Payis' winnings belonged to all children of the litigants, to be held for them in trust by the rabbinical court, who would oversee their equitable disbursal.

And what about the divorce? shouted the aggrieved R' Shaposhnikov, who had just come back from hospital to witness the very ending of the drama, whose final adjudication had not even been his. This apostate is breaking the Gershomite dictum! We cannot let him scoff at Jewish Law!

R' Amatzia, who had already begun to pack his pillow, said over his shoulder, I hereby permit Nathan Berkovitch to stay married to both wives. Unless either wife wants a divorce?

No, said Miriam. I love him even though he's a bastard.

And I too, said Batya. Both things.

Me also, said Hadassah. Even though I can't marry him.

But, shouted R' Shaposhnikov, overcome once more, it is a grave sin he is living in! And, he added in a choked voice, it is a sin to rule against the Gershomite dictum!

A sin? So let it be a sin, R' Amatzian said, his mouth twisting. For the Torah's sake, I hereby take the sin upon myself.

And so saying, he folded his pillow, stuffed it into his travel bag, and left the courtroom in a wide-legged limp.

Outside, as if by a miracle, a cab was already waiting.

Soon thereafter the matter died down. The Shleif-Berkovitch family returned to its Haifa apartment in HaBonim Street, #13, and within a year all women bore more children. Miriam bore twin boys, and invited the Second Luminescence to their circumcision ceremony. But R' Amatzia had died soon after the trial, and so R' Shaposhnikov was the godfather instead—people said he had not wanted to come, but was ordered to (some say by the Prime Minister himself), for the sake of reconciliation.

Who was the new children's father, you ask, Nathan or Jacob? What difference does it make, so long as the children received food and love, and were taught Torah and arithmetic and to be kind to others? What was important was that the children's family was not wrecked, and was even improved by the Payis' winnings. (Hadassah bought a piano.) And of course the Halacha was saved too, and so was the government coalition, because with the Torah Laws still valid, all yeshiva students, no matter what age, received free room and board at government expense, besides an exemption from military service, and also a healthy stipend. So healthy, in fact, that soon there were many more yeshiva students and more yeshivas had to be built, and taxes raised—including taxes on lottery winnings.

But this of course did not apply to Nathan's winning ticket—and luckily, too, because by that time, the Shleif-Berkovitch family's expenses had risen further, after Nathan had taken a second pilegesh (a rabbi's widow whom he had met during the court proceedings), and this one bore him two children. (The elder, who became a Shin Bett agent when he grew up, was the one who caught the truck loaded with explosives that nearly blew up the Knesset building with all members inside.)

Until they all moved to a house in Tel Aviv five years ago, the Shleif-Berkovitch family continued to live in the same Haifa apartment, where they also entertained my father when he came to visit and sometimes stayed the night.

But that's an entirely different mish-mash.

Curse

After his second wife died also from cancer, my Uncle Getzl left the Or HaNer Yeshiva in Bney Barak where my mother was paying for him to learn Mishna and Talmud under a grand nephew of the Chazon Ish, and rented for himself a little room on the roof of No. 71 Shabazi Street, with only a mattress, and immediately began to study cancer from the Talmud and the Gmara and also the Poskim, to see if maybe he could find there something, in case he got married again it shouldn't happen next time also.

The first month, my mother came every day to Shabazi and cried and said, Getzl you should go back and finish to study in the Yeshiva, because maybe it's all from God and we shouldn't ask why. But Getzl said that cancer was only from Ashmedai, and he, Getzl, was going to find out how, to teach the Evil One a lesson, what it means to take two wives from one man one after the other. When my mother heard this, she said he (Getzl) should not speak like this, or he could go too after the wives, he had a full life ahead of him, he was only 43 maybe, that's young. But Getzl did not listen to her, so finally my father said, Leave him alone, maybe after a month he'll go back, and even if not, it's cheaper in Shabazi than in the Yeshiva. So then they (my father and my mother) had a big fight, and finally my mother called a taxi to bring Rabbi Guthelf from Bney Barak special to Shabazi (it cost nineteen *Lirot*). But nothing came out of it, because Getzl did not even open the door and just said from behind it to leave him alone with his grief, which is what he also said to the matchmaker, that my mother brought the next week, just in case he got interested. So finally finally that's what they did. Nobody came, and every week I had to go to Shabazi to bring for Getzl something to eat so he wouldn't die from hunger.

At first, when I came to bring to him to eat (some tchulent that my mother sent or maybe soup, or a piece of boiled chicken with far-fel), I saw that he not only got thinner every day, but also more white from staying all the time in the inside of the room and only read-ing. So, like my mother asked me, I tried to talk to him, to see if he wanted something else maybe, or a fish, or maybe a challah, but Getzl said he did not want anything, or to talk to anybody, and he only made big sighs and said Ruchale, Ruchale my innocent treas-ure, Ashmedai should have taken me instead of you. (Ruchale is the name of Getzl's second wife that died from cancer, in the stomach.) But after two months, because I always stayed until he finished to eat, to take the plates and the pot back (so he wouldn't put the cigarette ash inside), Getzl began to talk from other things, which usually was cancer, and cancer, and more cancer, all from the Bible and the Talmud and also the Mishna, like I said, and how he was going to find everything out, but I didn't understand much, because this was three years ago, and I was only maybe ten, before my Bar Mitzvah even.

Now I have to stop and explain, because it's not really true what I said before, that Getzl only had a mattress in his room, because he also had an old bookshelf with books that he took from the Yeshiva in Bney Barak (or maybe they gave him, I don't know), and he also had three orange boxes that were once empty but that he filled with the copybooks where he wrote what he found about cancer in the Bible and the Talmud and the Mishna, like I said. So when I stayed to take the pots back, every time it was the same thing: first he offered me a Dubek cigarette, even that he knew my mother did not let me smoke (in the Yeshiva everyone does), then after I put the pot and the plates on the ice box where he ate from like a table, he took out from an orange box the copybook where he wrote what he read about the cancer, and told me the last things he just found, which if the doctors only listened to him, they would know about the cancer everything, and also maybe what to do, and then Ashmedai would have a *feig*.

For example, there was this Mitzvah with the Red Cow's ash from Deuteronomy, which the Grand Priest in the days of the Temple had to burn when there was a pestilence (if the people sinned, or even if not) and throw it (the ash) in the wind to stop the pestilence. And why? All because (that's what Getzl found in the Mishna) the ash could heal like an ointment or sulfa, from America, which his first wife at first also got. And why? Because everything if it could cause sickness, it could also heal it if it was done in the opposite way and not so much. Of this even *Rashi* knew, which was a big proof, because *Rashi* not only invented the *Rashi* script to write his explanations from the Bible and the Talmud in secret from the Goyim, but he also wrote explanations to the Rambam, who was the private doctor of the King of Egypt before *Rashi* was even born, or even the Malbim or the Radak, who also (both of them) wrote explanations to the Bible and the Talmud. So that's also a big point.

Anyway, this is what my Uncle Getzl found and this is what he told not only to me, but also to Doctor Pesach Rivkin, from Hadassah Hospital, because he (Dr. Rivkin) wrote an article in the newspaper *Ma'ariv* (page eleven) about cancer so that everyone would understand, in simple Hebrew. That's why Getzl wrote to him (Dr. Rivkin), because *Ma'ariv* is the only thing not in Yiddish that he reads sometimes, besides the Bible and the Talmud, like I said, and also the Mishna.

So Getzl wrote to him (Dr. Rivkin) that the cancer comes from ash, like from the Red Cow in the Pentateuch, which is clear not just from *Rashi* and the Radak, but also from the Mishna, and this is why to kill the cancer you also need to use ash, but in the opposite way, even if nobody knows how yet, and even if in the beginning it makes you a little sick, if you put in too much, because what's a little sickness if you want to cure the cancer? That's what my Uncle Getzl said he found, and that's what he told to Dr. Rivkin, in the letter. But the problem was, first of all, that Dr. Rivkin maybe didn't get the letter, and even if he did, that his secretary maybe didn't give it to him because she didn't understand about this, or maybe also from jealousy that he shouldn't listen to someone else, only to her. So this was the first problem. And the second problem was that Getzl didn't know how to write in Hebrew too exactly, so from shame he wrote to Dr. Rivkin in Yiddish, and maybe he (Dr. Rivkin) didn't know Yiddish, or maybe his secretary didn't know. So that's the second problem, and that's why he (Getzl) sent him (Dr. Rivkin) another letter, in Hebrew, which I had to help him to write, with everything from what he found. And from this letter the big problem started.

It started because after maybe a month, Dr. Rivkin wrote again in *Ma'ariv* (page fourteen) and said he just wrote to England an opinion that maybe cancer is from food and from smoking, and to cure it of course first you have to change the food and no smoking, but also maybe you have to drink special medicine like poison, that kills the cancer from the inside, which came from it first, nobody can know if it works or not until they tried.

So that's how it all started, because of this second article, and what happened was this: On Saturday morning in seven o'clock someone banged on the door of our apartment on Klonimus Street and shouted so loud, he almost woke up all the neighbours, and Mr. Farbel from downstairs even called the police (but luckily they didn't want to come just because of noise, it happened before). Finally my father opened the door, and before he could say Shabat Shalom, he (Getzl) rushed in and shouted at my mother (in the kitchen) that he wanted to take this Dr. Rivkin before a court, he (Dr. Rivkin) should be ashamed from what he had done, and also pay him (Getzl) damages for stealing his thinking, which he (Getzl) found all by himself from the Talmud and Rashi.

When he finished shouting and he sat down, my mother first gave Getzl to drink and a towel to wipe his face, then my father explained to him that a lawyer would cost him maybe fifteen *Lirot* an hour before he opened up his mouth even, so Getzl said all right, he'll take Dr. Rivkin to Din Torah, before the biggest Rabbis in Tel Aviv, he knew two of them from the Yeshiva in Bney Barak, so it was a big advantage from his side, and also he (Getzl) could speak there by himself without fifteen *Lirot*, because they (the Rebbes) knew Yiddish. But then it all of a sudden came out from my mother that she just remembered someone told her this Dr. Rivkin was a well known Atheist, so maybe he wouldn't even come when the Rabbis sent for him, it happened before. So did they need this, someone like him reducing their honour? And all because of Getzl?

So finally finally, after Getzl ate some chopped egg salad (with onion) and also some honeycake with Nescafé (half milk), he said that Rebbes or no Rebbes, never in the world will he forget from it, what Dr. Rivkin did to him, and Dr. Rivkin shouldn't think he (Getzl) will just pass on it just like that, without doing something to give him (Rivkin) back something, for all the grief he (Getzl Goldman) got from him, after he gave to him everything he found, for free.

My father then said that whatever Getzl had in mind sounded better than court or Din Torah, and he (my father) was happy he (Getzl) was using his head finally, and then he shook his hand. Then after he (Getzl) left (he took some honey cake in a newspaper, for Shabazi), my father said, See? You just have to talk to him like a normal human being.

But he (my father) didn't know what he started, because next time I went to bring to Getzl something to eat (half a klops with sliced boiled egg inside, and also some calf-foot jelly, also with eggs inside), I saw that he had put all the Talmud and Mishna books in the corner under a piece of cloth, and he was sitting on the floor with some other books around him, from leather, it came out these were from the Kabbalah, I don't know where he got them, but probably from someone in the Yeshiva, they have to hide them anyway, in case the Rebbe will catch them, and then they'll have to say *Shma' Yisra'el* a hundred times, so why not give them to Getzl.

At first he didn't want to say why he got the leather books, but finally after he ate the klops (I also brought him some horse radish) it finally came out the reason he got them was because he was putting a big curse on Dr. Rivkin, after what he (Dr. Rivkin) did to him, even if it was only the *klafte* secretary, because he (Rivkin) was responsible.

Now I have to stop and say on the side that I was personally myself very interested in this, because all the curses I knew how to say were small little curses in Arabic, like *Kus Emaq*, which is (begging your pardon) Your mother's cunt, and *Yechrebetaq*, which is May your house fall down, and also one or two small curses to say in Yiddish that I don't know what they mean. But even when I said them all together seven times, with the name of Raffi Buchholtz that used to throw sand on my hair, nothing happened, he only threw more sand, and also when Ruthy Levin was watching. So when I heard this, I asked Getzl if I could maybe learn one or two small curses from him, from what he read in the Kabbalah, in case I would need them sometime for who knows what. But Getzl said no-one should curse just like that, without a big reason, because curses can sometimes bring up from the Tophet black angels and damaged spirits and other ruiners, so if you weren't careful and didn't know how to do it exactly exactly like the books from the Kabbalah said, like for example washing seven times in the *Mikveh* and saying *Shehecheyanu* prayer eighteen times, and other things that he didn't even want to talk about, because it was all secret, then if you didn't do all these things, maybe the curse would turn around and jump on your head, so then go get rid of it, and who needs it? Nobody. So that's why he didn't let me read in the books from leather, and only told me for a favour what he was going to wish upon Dr. Rivkin's head, that he deserved everything which he would get, because of the big grief he gave to others.

So that's the first thing. Then second, he (Getzl) wished boils (*parech*, in Yiddish) upon Dr. Rivkin's whole body, like the *Sh'chin* in the Haggadah from Passover, that the Egyptians got after they said No to God, and this he (Getzl) asked not from cruelty, but only so he (Rivkin) should know how he (Getzl) felt all over the body when he (Getzl) saw in the *Ma'ariv* (page fourteen) what Dr. Rivkin wrote, without saying even one word how it all came from Getzl and what he (Getzl) found in the Mishna all by himself. So that's second.

But then the third and the biggest thing, Getzl said, he especially asked Ashmedai himself (which if he did this, he, Getzl, promised not to find about the cancer) to make Dr. Rivkin so he can't make children to his wife in case he had a wife, which Getzl didn't know if he had, or from the *klafte* secretary in case this was the one he wanted to get married with. And this third was the biggest biggest thing because (Getzl said) if a man couldn't make children to his wife she completely lost all the respect for him from the wedding and didn't wash or cook or even speak politely with him. So this would be the biggest result if everything happened like he (Getzl) asked.

When I heard all this I was very interested, like I said, and I wanted to stay to see how Getzl asked these questions from Ashmedai, even if Raffi Buchholtz said he didn't want to get married with Ruthy Levin, just in case he changed his mind. But then I had to go home with the pot and the plates so I couldn't stay, and I forgot to tell everything to my mother, because on the way back I had to go around, not to meet Raffi (for the last week he was trying to catch me, because of what I told about to him to Ruthy, even if it was all true, that he didn't want to get married with her.) So this is why I forgot to tell my mother about Getzl and the curses he was going to wish on the head of Dr. Rivkin, and that's why it was really my fault what happened later, because my mother had adjured me to tell her everything that her Meshiggene brother said when I went to bring to him to eat.

Finally when I told her (the next day) what Getzl said, about the curses, she stamped with her foot on the floor and said to my father (this was at night right after he came back from the shoe store), Come with me we're going to talk to this Shmeggegge and take him back to the Yeshiva I don't care if I have to tie him up with my own hands. My father said he wasn't going anywhere especially Friday night before he ate, because without eating he couldn't do anything, especially later. But my mother said there was going to be no later if he didn't come right now, and then I said I wanted to come too. Oh sure, my father said, let's take the neighbours also, so they can all see what family I got married with, and then there was a big fight with shouting. But finally my mother cried, so my father put on his black sandals and said All right, all right, just for you Malkah, and we took bus No. 12 to Shabazi and climbed all the stairs to the roof to see Getzl, and to take him back to the Yeshiva.

This was maybe eight o'clock in the night and the light in the hall didn't work, so it was Egyptian darkness, like it says in the Haggadah, and Getzl's bell also didn't work. So my father knocked and knocked, but there was no answer from anybody, so he said maybe he (Getzl) is asleep, this Smeggegge, from all the klops and tzimes. But my mother said He's not asleep, we would hear him snoring from downstairs (this is true), there is no noise from the inside of the room. So finally my mother took out the key that once she made a copy from Getzl's own key that Katchalski the landlord gave to her, and opened the door.

Immediately we got in I could smell such a smell like a stink worse than a dead cat or (begging your pardon) an outhouse in a Moshav, but we could see nothing, only Getzl sitting on the floor like an Arabush, with the legs crossed but the eyes open. My father went to him and said (begging your pardon), Getzl, Getzl, you farted all the klops? but he (Getzl) didn't move, so my father looked and looked, but the stink came from I don't know where. My mother rightaway ran to open the window and the other door that goes to the roof where all the other people that live in Shabazi No. 71 hang the laundry, and immediately a big black cat tried to get in, but my father said Kisht! Kisht! and my mother said, I adjure you! and finally the cat left. Then she put Getzl on the mattress and with the broom she cleaned up all the pieces of paper on the floor, half of them burnt (on his head Getzl had burns too), and my father said, Go downstairs to Katchalski and say Isser (that's the name of my father) asks please for a half cup of maybe cognac or even cherry brandy, something strong. So I went down but I came back only with a quarter bottle of Carmel benediction wine (Katchalski said he didn't have something else), and my father said, It's even better. Then with the knife for the bread he opened Getzl's teeth and my mother poured the wine into his mouth. And then this is what happened, believe me because I am not lying:

First Getzl sat up like with a spring, then he shouted like a rooster two times, and finally when my father said, Getzl, I adjure you (my father never said this before, only my mother, because he said it's superstition for old wives), Getzl began to say Shehecheyanu, that a Jew should say only after he wants to say Thanks to God. But then (I heard it with my own ears) he also began to say HaGomel, which is what a Jew should pray (but he doesn't have to) if he got saved from mortal danger not from his own effort. My father tried to stop him and said, It's not for this, but my mother said Let him.

And then came the thing which I don't know how to tell, because my mother and father adjured me not to tell to anybody, so I'll only say that he (Getzl) became all wet in the pants. And he also began to cry from the eyes and the nose, and said he made a big sin, he should ask forgiveness in Yom Kippur. So finally we took him to downstairs, to Shabazi Street, then (Katchalski called a taxi already) to Hadassah Hospital on Balfour Street (luckily it's always open).

And now comes the best part, because who do you think was in the hospital in the night shift? I knew you'd say this, and you are right: Dr. Pesach Rivkin, that it came out he was also from Warsaw like my father, only he went to Auschwitz and my father only to Maidanek, and that's why they never met, but my father met his mother's cousin, in a Bar Mitzvah in Haifa. So he (Dr. Rivkin) said What have we here? The genius almost-Rebbe that sends me annotations to the Mishna in Yiddish how to cure the cancer and also diabetes? So Getzl said I never said diabetes, I only said cancer, and diabetes only maybe. Then he again cried from the eyes and the nose even more, and rightaway you could see he was sorry and regretted what he (Getzl) asked from Ashmedai about Dr. Rivkin, because he (Dr. Rivkin) was with only one eye and the left hand didn't move so good, it was probably from the Camps, so why add to his troubles, just because he had a secretary *klafte*? Also he (Rivkin) was already bald in the head worse than Getzl and he also spoke to him in Yiddish, so immediately you could see he was a good doctor that you can talk with him. (That's what my mother said later.) And to make it worse, it came out that Getzl's father (that's my grandfather Menachem-Leizer that went with Hitler) also was a good friend from the Cheder of Dr. Rivkin's brother. So when it came out all this, Getzl stood on the bed and shouted Upon my own head all I've wished upon the heads of the innocents! But then he had to lie down because everybody (also the two nurses) and my father and mother included, made him do it, and then a nurse gave him a little injection (I don't want to say where), and after this we left.

The next day, in the morning (it was a Saturday) we all came to visit but Getzl was in a different room, with a tube made from plastic going into his pyjama pants, he should not make his pants wet again, and bandages on his head because of the burns he got from the burnt paper, and also on his face, he could only eat maybe a little mashed potatoes, so what my mother brought, all the gefilte fish and the tzimes and the compote, my father said Good, now we can eat it, but my mother said No, she'll give it to Dr. Rivkin, he'll eat some and give the rest to poor sick people that don't have family. So then my father said Malkah (that's my mother's name), my treasure, where did I find you, and Dr. Rivkin (he just came in) said Nu, this you can do at home. So to make a long story short, that's why I didn't get to learn any curses from my Uncle Getzl, who after three days in the hospital ran away in the night back to Or HaNer Yeshiva, and after this he didn't want to say anything about curses when I asked him (except that nobody should say them). But because I went to clean his room and to take the leather books back to the Yeshiva, I read in one of them all about how to put a curse on someone that tries to take from you something, and maybe after Passover I'll try it.

Talking to the Enemy

Before Kol Israel radio had even reported it, Nitza called me from the kibbutz and said that there had been a disaster: three terrorists had sneaked in and had barricaded themselves in the children's nursery. "They . . . they are there right now," she said, her voice cracking.

I swept all papers off my desk, including the insurance form I was filling for the new client, who now sat before me, his eyebrows joined in displeasure.

"Is Ilan there, inside?" I asked.

Ilan was our five-year-old boy. He had remained with Nitza in the kibbutz after we had divorced, three years before, when I moved back to Tel Aviv.

"Y . . . yes," Nitza said, her harsh weeping echoing through the long distance crackle.

"I'm coming," I said.

I knew I wouldn't make it in time—it was three-and-a-half hours away to Kibbutz Sha'anan—it's almost on the border with

Lebanon—but all I could think of was that last week it had been my turn to have Ilan, and that I had cancelled because I had work to do.

"Where you going?" asked the client. He was an old yekke, a German Jew, who had come to have his jewellery store insured. (I had opened an insurance agency, after I had left the army.)

"I must go," I told him.

"Now?"

Without answering I grabbed my car keys, and, like an idiot, also the .22 Beretta from my desk drawer (only in the car did I see that the magazine was empty), and ran out.

All the way north I kept thinking that maybe if I drove fast I could still get there in time, not allowing myself to think anything else. But when I arrived at the kibbutz it was of course over.

Whether the rescue attempt was botched, or whether there had never been any chance of success, was never made clear, and was really irrelevant. The moment the three terrorists had raced through the old almond orchard, passing Chanan Berkovitch, the old Bible teacher, on their way in, it seemed almost pre-ordained. Sweeping by him, they shouted—in Hebrew, no less—that it was a military exercise, and the fool—he was returning from guard duty at the avocado field, with a loaded Uzi and two magazines, a walkie-talkie, everything—the fool let them pass; even with their Russian RPGs slung plainly across their backs, with the Syrian-green ammo boxes they were lugging between them as they ran, with the AK-47 Kalashnikovs swinging at their hips—even with all this, he let them pass.

But a moment later, when there was a shot and the children started screaming inside the nursery (the fuckers had killed the teacher, Miryam Goldin, with a single bullet to the head the moment they burst in), everybody knew, and all men raced pell-mell to the rescue, grabbing whatever they could find: Uzis, Kalashs, MAC-10s, Gallils, even rusty Mausers and British Lee Enfields that were stashed in the armoury somewhere, from the days of '48.

The terrorists (no-one knew yet how many there were, three or four) had in the meantime barricaded themselves in the nursery, pushing cribs and beds against the swinging doors, and began shooting out the windows without pause. They must have brought thousands of rounds of ammo with them, probably in their backpacks, too. The first to get it was Chanan Berkovitch—he rushed ahead as if asking for it—then Micha Barzel, the manager of the cowshed with whom I used to play ping-pong, and by that time a patrol of Golani that was in the area, mapping some *wadi*, took over until the *Sayeret*, the recon commando, arrived by helis from Ramat David. It took them only 40 minutes, I'll give them that.

Later I was told that of the nine children, two had probably died right after the fuckers had bound them too tightly, or something. The three had brought with them large spools of copper wire, and pliers, for this. I didn't ask if Ilan was one of the two. What did it matter? When I arrived, the *Chevre Kadisha*, the burial society, was already there. The moment I saw them, three stooped old men with black skullcaps and flapping black coats through which the fringes of their prayer shawls flickered, I knew it, before I even saw them dragging the small coffins into the nursery, trampling over the asters.

"Don't go in!" Moosa Hartov shouted at me. He had been my second-in-command when I left the *Sayeret* two years before. He rushed to my side and grabbed my arm. "I'm telling you, don't go in!"

He was still dressed in the black Nomex coverall with the kevlar vest, and with the tight kevlar helmet on his head, looking like a fancy spaceman with all these objects hanging from his back and belt, radios, flares, magazines, syringes, knives, nylon ropes, clusters of grenades. He smelled of cordite and blood, his Patuga canvas boots grimy with blood and brains.

I tried to push by him but he stiff-armed me away. Four medics stumbled by, carrying three soldiers piled on one stretcher, all dead. One soldier had his neck torn off and the head lolled on to the side, hanging by a thread of skin. His mouth moved. Then the medic slapped it back onto the stretcher and threw a grey blanket over the corpses.

The crowd of kibbutzniks stood frozen, whispering in shock. Only the crackle of radios and the slow whirr of the heli blades could be heard, and a distant chirp of some sprinklers, probably at the avocado fields.

Nitza stood a little way off, her red hair flying in all directions, hands to her mouth, with Yossi, this husband of hers, at her side. He carried a ridiculously long Nagant, a Russian pistol as long as his thigh and older than he, 50 years old, maybe. He probably got to the armoury last and that's all that was left. Both she and he were in pyjamas. They were probably in bed, screwing, when it happened.

"I came as soon as I could," I said.

Nitza rattled her head violently from side to side, as if saying, "Don't talk to me."

Her husband said that it had just ended. "They got them all," he said. "Finally."

"But the children?" I asked. I couldn't see how we could talk so quietly. The sun was shining on the wet grass, from somewhere came a merry tune from a forgotten radio. The sprinklers still chirped.

"Nine of the eleven," Yossi said. "Nine. Also Ilan." He began to curse in Arabic, at length. I couldn't see what this would accomplish now, cursing.

Nitza chose that moment to start screaming, and at the sound of her voice all the other women began to screech, too. I looked at her and all at once, without thinking, I turned around and barged in, pushing Moosa aside. This time he said nothing and let me pass.

The inside of the nursery looked like a broken dollhouse splashed with ketchup. There was more red than white on the walls. Two unshaven hippies, their black t-shirts spattered with dark brown, were slumped against an overturned crib, under a large cardboard drawing of the Evil Haman leading the Virtuous Mordechai on a horse, with Queen Esther looking on. The holiday of Purim was two days away and the older children had probably made this drawing for the younger ones, for the party. Soon they would have begun making them their Purim masks. The two terrorists looked calm, as if sleeping. Grey stuff dripped from their heads. A third one was lying face down in the door, his head a mass of red and yellowish grey. In the other room the three Kadishers were bending over some small heaps. I began going in their direction but at that moment Moosa caught up with me and dragged me back by my belt, with both hands.

"Don't be a donkey," he hissed.

I heard myself ask "PLF?"

The Palestine Liberation Front had a training camp in Lebanon, not 30 miles away, in the Bik'aa. Twice before they had tried to get in, but each time a Golani patrol got them. Now they didn't.

"No, PLO. They had their papers on."

The three Kadishers went by, single file, each carrying a little box. I made to follow them but Moosa, one hand still at my belt, hit softly at my jaw with the open palm of his other hand, turning my head away.

"No," he said.

I said, "I want in on the retribution."

"Don't be a donkey," Moosa said, released my belt, and was gone.

In a second he was back. He punched my shoulder, hard. "Mother's cunt," he said. "They got three of my guys, too."

He again grabbed my belt, and this time I let him pull me out; on the way I saw the Kadishers going in again. Outside, on the grass, were six cardboard boxes, not very large.

"I want in on this," I said.

"They got them with RPGs through the walls."

But I couldn't care about this, now.

"I want in."

"Your mother's cunt. Once you are out, you are out!"

I opened my mouth to argue, but just then the Prime Minister arrived, and the reporters, in two large Super Frelons, and also a Cobra Medevac, with a red Magen David on its tail. The Prime Minister nodded at me, curtly. He used to visit our apartment in Tel Aviv, and talk to my father in the kitchen, over tea glasses.

Yaro Peleg, the Chief of Staff, stood beside him.

He said to the PM, "The fuckers got three of ours, also, in the first two minutes, with RPGs."

Someone behind said that the terrorists had wanted to bargain, as usual. The kids, for some imprisoned Fatach-guys. "But don't they know by now? That we never talk to them?"

The PM asked, "Our guys had these American suits on? That cost us $500 each? Now look at this." He gestured with both hands toward the empty stretchers flapping on the Cobra's skids, in the rotor's wash.

"It can only stop 7.62 mm," the Chief of Staff said, abashed. "Maybe 9 mm."

The PM looked at me.

"Yes," I said. "Maximum."

There was a short pause. The reporters began to inch forward.

"How's your father?" the Prime Minister said.

"Alive," I said. "My son got it."

He nodded, his mouth pinched, and immediately turned on his heels and left. He probably knew I was going to ask him the same thing I had asked of Moosa.

I didn't get to see either Nitza, or Ilan's body, or any of the other bereaved parents, before I returned to Tel Aviv. I only sat down for a few minutes with her husband, Yossi, who said he'll see about everything, and would let me know about the funeral.

It was painful for both of us, this conversation; the betrayed husband and the new husband, the winning fornicator. But we made the most of it, like civilized people. He brewed coffee, and I didn't find it in me to refuse. I was amazed how numb I felt. Nine children dead, one of them mine, three old friends also, and all I felt was a sort of odd heat inside my stomach, and a tingling inside my nose. No tears; nothing.

I asked Yossi, belatedly, whether any of his own children got it, too.

"No," he said. "Thank God. Last month, they transferred to the children's house." His freckled face vibrated as if a fan was blowing air through his skin, from the inside.

The children's house was for kids six and up.

"That's good," I said.

He, too, had been married, when Nitza and he began screwing behind my back, when I was away in Egypt, or in Jordan, in deep penetrations, or in ambushes, and two of the children from his first marriage, the twins, were still in the kibbutz, both boys. The third, a girl, left with her mother, to live in Haifa.

He offered me to stay with them, in the spare bedroom. Nitza had been born in the kibbutz and thus had privileges: it was a two-room house, with a kitchenette too. Before Yossi moved in I used to live there, with her.

"No," I said, "I must go back."

He didn't even try to convince me to stay.

I don't recall anything of the trip back. I think a policeman on a motorcycle caught up with me just after Haifa. But I told him something, showed him some of my old papers, and he let me go.

Back in Tel Aviv I called my father. He was 72 then, and no longer active in anything, but still had his contacts, from the Army, and the government, where he was once a minister without portfolio, "for shmutz," as he had said once. Dirty things.

"I heard it," he said. "Ilan went."

I said they got all the fuckers, finally. "But I am sure they'll do something, to retaliate."

"Sure they will," said my father. In his younger days he had been one of the founders of the *Sayeret*, in a way.

"I want in," I said.

"How's Nitza?" my father asked.

His calm in disasters used to infuriate me, but by now I was used to it. Or maybe I was growing to be more like him. It's not something to be proud of. Sometimes I wish I could scream, too. My only son just got it, and not one tear.

"She's so-so," I said.

"Yossi with her?"

When I didn't answer he said, "Nu, *baruch dayan emett.*" Blessed be the True Judge. A Jew is supposed to say this after someone had died; to show he is not mad at God, or anything.

I said, "I want in on this."

"Don't be a donkey," my father said. "Leave this to them."

"I am not old yet," I said. "I want in on this. Call Dada, tell him I want to."

David Shlomovitz was the current commander of the *Sayeret*, another Tel Aviv boy. He had been three classes below me, in Alliance high school, in Ramat Aviv. Used to play the violin, too, and also soccer.

"You go to sleep, Mickey," my father said. "Tomorrow we'll go together to see Nitza. You want me to drive?"

I said I didn't want him to drive; I didn't want to see Nitza. I wanted in on the Retribution Operation.

My father said, "Even if I called, they'd never take you, you know that. You didn't do what you were told, the last time."

"This time I'll do anything," I said.

Two years before, I had left the *Sayeret*—was let go, really—after refusing to give the go-ahead in a little RO, in Lebanon. Two months it had taken to plan. A local chieftain of the Hizbollah, a good mechanic, who specialized in delayed Katyusha rockets. All his sons helped him, all six of them, none older than eleven. We were outside his yard already, but he had three of them seated on his knees. Maybe he knew we were near. I took everybody back. Two of my guys got it, on the way back, from snipers. Finally a sniper of ours, from the paratroopers recon, got him.

"No," said my father. "You can come here, if you want, you can sleep in your old bed." And he hung up.

I called Dada Shlomovitz myself, at his home in Tzahala, north of Tel Aviv, where all the married officers lived. He picked up the phone on the first ring.

"It's Mickey," I said.

"No," he said. "I talked to Moosa. I . . . I am sorry about Ilan, but no."

He said a few other things, about Ilan, and about Nitza, and how in a month or something he would come to see me, if I wanted, when everything was over.

He didn't specify what would be over, and I didn't have to ask. In the background I could hear several men's voices, gruff, curt, talking in low tones. No women.

I said, "I speak French, Arabic, come on, Dada."

"No. I said no."

There was a pause. I knew I was being foolish. This was an open phone line.

"Please," I said. "In this, I must—"

He hung up.

Next morning my father called. I put the album with Ilan's old photos back in the drawer and we spoke for a while about nothing. The heat, the synagogue where he was now a committee member (he had inexplicably become religious, when my mother died, two years before), my failing insurance brokerage business. Suddenly, out of the blue, he said, "Get married again, you donkey, you can have more children."

I told him I didn't need his advice.

"I talked to Moosa," he said, as if continuing the same line of conversation. "They are afraid to take you, you never do what you are told."

What did they mean never? Only once. I said, "I'll swear on the grave of anyone they want."

"I tried," my father said.

Later on he came by, and we went together in his Lark to his synagogue on Bugrashov Street, where he had prayed off and on since he had arrived in Palestine, 52 years before, and where Nitza and I, against the surly objections of the other kibbutzniks (who didn't hold with religious meddling in civilian affairs) were married six years before, under the ancient joumes trees in the yard. We

were divorced in Haifa three years later, by some Yemenite Rabbi
who first tried to reconcile us, without success, for two hours.

The synagogue was hot and dusty, and nearly empty, in such a
mid-week day (it was a Tuesday, I think). Even the Rabbi was away.
But we finally collared eight more men, from Bugrashov Street, for
a minyan, merchants from the area, a cobbler, two tailors, a kiosk
owner, and several old men who had been dozing on the park bench.

I repeated the Kaddish prayer clumsily after my father, reading
it over his shoulder in his frayed Siddur. I hadn't even known you
could say the Kaddish before the funeral. So many funerals I had
been to, I never even paid attention to the prayers anymore.

After the service was over (my father thanked the others one by
one, earnestly, as if they had done him a very great favour) we got
into his ancient Lark and he drove me home. All during the
Kaddish neither he nor I had shed a tear. I don't know if it's normal or not; that's the way it was. When my mother died, he didn't
cry either, only I did, a little. But this was just after I had been let
go from the *Sayeret*, so I don't know whether it was for her that I
cried, or for the shame of what had happened to me, in the Army,
how I failed her, and him.

He dropped me off in Keren Kayemet Boulevard, at the rooftop
apartment that I was then renting. Before I got out of the car he
clasped my neck, loosely, in his old thin hand, and said into my
cheek, "Get married again, you'll have other kids, as many as you
want. Thirty-eight is not old, thirty-eight. . . ." and suddenly he began
to weep, the tears dropping down his hook nose, fat and oily and clear.

I struggled free and asked him in embarrassment whether he
wanted to come up.

"No," he said, wiping his eyes. "I want to go to sleep."

After my mother's death he had also wanted to sleep all the
time, only sleep.

We sat a few more minutes in his old Lark, awkwardly silent, while outside, along Keren Kayemet Boulevard, marauding children in masks and costumes banged on cars with plastic hammers. Pirates, cowboys, and little Arabs. It was the eve of Purim, and Purim parties for children were everywhere.

After my father had driven off I went straight to my car and drove to Tzahala to see Dada Shlomovitz.

There was the usual white Subaru, with its windows curtained, parked at the entrance of his small villa, under the *tzaftzafa* trees. As I emerged out of my Taunus the Subaru's door opened and a young Moroccan got out, his right hand at the back of his belt. He seemed vaguely familiar, but I couldn't place him. But he, apparently, knew me. Probably someone from the Shin-Bett, with whom I had worked before on something. There were so many things, I couldn't remember them all, nor did I want to.

"Oh, *shalom* Mickey," he said, lamely. "I . . . I heard about it, about your boy. . . . You going to see Dada?"

I nodded and climbed the bare concrete stairs. The door wasn't even locked. Inside the living-room were Dada and Moosa, talking and waving their hands in the air, and three other men. Yaro Peleg, the chief of staff, tall and thickset, and two others, one short and bald, the other tall and curly, leaning on the wall. Probably *shoo-shoo*: Shin Bett or Mossad. New guys. A lot had changed in the last few years, after the fuck-up of '73, and I haven't kept in touch.

Moosa and Dada stopped talking. "What you doing here?" Dada snapped.

I sat down on a chair without being invited.

One of the *shoo-shoo*s said, "That's Mickey BenAtar?"

"*Hada hoo,*" Dada said in Arabic. That's him.

"I want in on this," I said.

Another man came in through the kitchen door, looked in, and went back to the kitchen.

I said, "You are shy three guys now, anyway."

"Four," Yaro said. "One died an hour ago."

"So you have a few vacancies," I said.

Moosa spread his arms wide at Dada, as if saying, "I tried," or "I told you."

Dada looked at me and shook his head. "There's no way I'll—"

At that moment the phone rang and Yaro picked it up. After a minute of grunting into it he put it down.

There was a pause. "Your mother's cunt, Mickey," he said. "What do you want from my life."

"Who was it?" said the taller *shoo-shoo*.

"Himself," said Yaro, looking at me. "Your father called him too."

I said once more I wanted in on the operation, like a broken record.

The shorter *shoo-shoo* man said maybe I'd better leave; I said No, and he said I'd better, and then I said he could try and make me— just like two idiot kids in a Tel Aviv schoolyard. "Yes I will," he said, and Yaro told him to keep his hands to himself, that I was a bereaved father, and other such shit.

I tried to squeeze some tears out, but none came, so I lowered my head and tried to pretend I was trying to hide my weeping. There was some shouting, between the two *shoo-shoo* guys and Dada, and then Moosa joined in, and the Chief of Staff too, who said it was up to Dada. At last Dada said, "But you never do what you are told."

"Once," I said. "Only once."

I could see I was in, so if they wanted me to grovel, all right, I would. I had said I would do anything.

"Two guys," Dada said. "One of them a sergeant, with three children himself. And for what? For a couple of fucking baby *Arabushim*? They'll grow up, they'll get RPGs themselves, for their birthdays."

"I speak Arabic and French," I said, "if you are going to Tunis."

"You are fat now," Moosa said. I could see I was in.

"Your mother's cunt is fat," I said. Now that I was in I could say anything I wanted.

"Your own mother's cunt," Dada shouted. "Your own mother's cunt! You are not the only bereaved father in the world."

"Yes," said the shorter *shoo-shoo*, tightly.

There was another short pause, of a different quality.

"I'll be in Chod HaKiddon tomorrow noon," I said.

"Tonight," said Moosa. "Your mother's cunt, tonight."

The other man came from the kitchen with a tray of five coffees. Dada said, "Tomorrow, after the funeral, is good enough." Stiffly he offered me a cup. But I saw they were itching to talk about me, so I refused, and left.

The funeral took place the following day in the small cemetery of Kibbutz Sha'anan. Nine little coffins, none larger than a big ammo box, and three large ones, one for Chanan Berkovitch, one for Micha Barzel and one for Miryam Goldin. I stood near Nitza all during the Kaddish, my father at her other side, Yossi, her husband, behind her, as if she was about to bolt and we had to hem her in. Yossi was dressed in his blue Air Force uniform, with all his medals and campaign decorations. He had been a Mirage pilot. A good one, I am told. My father and I came in civilian clothes.

As the coffins were being lowered into the graves (a whole platoon of Golani had arrived, and they lowered them all at once, on order, with ropes), Nitza said, "You going with them, to Tunis?"

I didn't even ask her how she knew there was going to be an operation. She was no longer with the *shoo-shoo*, but so what. She only had to ask.

I hoisted my shoulder, to indicate a Maybe.

"If you want me there, I'll go too."

"No no," my father said. "We have enough people."

Yossi said something, behind us. About keeping our voices down.

"So get them," she said, not indicating whether she had meant get all our people, or get cracking and go get the fuckers who had done this.

"Yes," she said after a while. "I'm finished with this. You go."

Nitza used to be stationed in the Mossad's Beirut office. That's how we had met; on the Beirut beach. She had been in charge of the car convoy that was supposed to wait for us at the Mua'alamiya beach. I had come in with the naval commandos, as the specialist. Nothing came out of the operation that time—Intelligence had fucked up, as usual, and the guy we were after, some Libyan with plenty of Qadhafy's money who was going around trying to launch another Group, had gone to a whore for the night, or maybe to his family; something. So Nitza and I ended up waiting on the beach until just before dawn, side by side in a cramped overheated Peugeot, talking about jazz and movies and soccer, in French, in case someone overheard us. She was a kibbutznik, I from Tel Aviv. But she had played the piano, when she was young, I the violin, and after a month we were married. It lasted three years. She left the *shoo-shoo* and returned to the kibbutz, after Ilan was born, to work in the flower hot-houses, and I joined the kibbutz as a member. But I was rarely home, and soon she began screwing around. In the Mossad it's no big deal. That's how they release the stress, I am told. But I couldn't take it, so we got divorced, and I returned to Tel Aviv. At first I came every week to see Ilan, then every two weeks, and when a few months later they kicked me out of the *Sayeret*, after this fuck-up in Lebanon, I began to see Ilan less, maybe once a month. Also I had just begun then to sell insurance, to make a living, so it was hard to get away from Tel Aviv.

The funeral took no more than half an hour. When the cantor finished, the soldiers loaded wooden bullets and fired into the air, and that was that. As we were walking back, to the dining-room, Nitza said, "Moosa said it's Abu Salam, for sure, that it was his operation."

"Probably," I said.

"His son fucks with Arafat, that's how he got to be Chief of Operations."

"Well, he's not bad," I said, speaking professionally.

"No," she said. "He's good, kus emmo." His mother's cunt.

Afterwards Moosa gave me a lift back to Chod Hakiddon, the *Sayeret*'s base near Yerushalayim, where we would train for the next two weeks. A team of carpenters was already building a mock-up of Abu Salam's villa. Like most PLO bigwigs he lived in Sidi Bousseid, a posh suburb of Tunis, not far from the old port city of Carthage.

We divided into two teams this time, not three. Moosa was head of Team Bett, I head of Team Aleph. Dada had asked for a special dispensation to lead a team himself, but it was denied. By that time the confirmation had already come in that it was indeed Abu Salam's project, and the training went into high gear. We trained at night, and at odd hours during the day, when no satellites flew overhead. Every time a satellite would come by, the siren would sound and we would duck into the canteen, leaving two or three guys outside to kick a football around, taking turns at the ball.

Once my father arrived, stayed for the night, watched a whole round of test-runs, had a talk with Dada, then left in the morning without even talking to me. Whether he was in on the thing, or just came to watch, I couldn't tell. He was retired, after all. The PM came too, once, and the Chief of Staff, but not many others. Only two Ministers, Defense and Foreign. The first was for, the second against. Once I overheard them betting on the competition; the PM bet on Moosa's team, Defense and Foreign on mine.

The competition between the two teams lasted as usual to the last few days. We were supposed to get into the villa, take him down and come out in less than 30 seconds. The team that did it fastest without a screw-up would get the commission, the other would play backup in the street outside.

My team won, at 29.6 seconds; Moosa's team came in at 31.3. The idea of using two teams is that if one member of the take-down team gets sick or something, before the operation, you switch the entire team. You don't plug a fresh member into the house-team after all this training, when it finally began to click.

Five days before our departure, before the final competition, even, Moosa and Dada and I flew into Tunis, via Paris and Rome. Someone in the Mossad had picked up a rumour in a Tripoli bar, that maybe the Israelis would do something, so the PM wanted us to check the place ourselves, before we brought everybody in; to see if they had beefed up security, if there has been a leak. But there was nothing. We toured the suburb, taking pictures, accompanied by the Tunis Mossad chief, and the 2IC from Paris, who had come in, too. It was nice. Trees, shrubs, flowers. They certainly lived it up, those fuckers, with all this money they extorted from the Saudis, and the Kuwaitis. We saw Arafat's house, Abu El-Chol's too, the intelligence chief, and the villa of Abu Salam, a pink stucco shoebox on the corner of a side-street, with a good view of the sea. We returned to Tel Aviv two days before D-day, and went back into training, for the final competition.

After my team won, Moosa took me aside, and gave me a little talk. "I'll be just behind you," he said. "You hear? When you see him, do it."

I thought I was over it, by now, but apparently not. I felt myself going red in the neck. "I was in this when you were still in high school," I told him. I then said a few other things, dredging all his fuck-ups, from his training days, even before.

But he didn't recoil. "Not like with this sheikh in Lebanon. Children shmildren, women schwomen. You see him, you take him down."

"Sure, I'll take him down," I said, restraining myself. "What do you think, I am going for a picnic?"

"Children they'll kill here?" Moosa snarled at me, as if I myself had killed some children, a moment ago. "We'll cut their *zayin* and stuff it in their mouth, so they'll know. Children they'll kill here?"

"Go to sleep," I said.

"No, really." Moosa said. "They want to fight? Man-to-man? Okay. But children?"

"*Yallah*," I said. "Enough."

"Peace they want us to make with them? With these *cholerot*? You want to make peace with fuckers who kill children?"

"Not me," I said.

At last he went to sleep. Probably angry that his team had lost.

We left on a Friday night from Ashdod, the southernmost Mediterranean port in Israel. My father came to see us go, maybe also to see me. He looked lost, in his frayed khaki pants and sweat-soaked nylon shirt, among the piles of ammo boxes, dismantled heli parts, irritable naval commandos amidst their heaps of odd gear, and just plain staff officers from the *Q'irya* in Tel Aviv, who had come to see the culmination of their plan. There was also the obligatory Rabbi who stood to the side, wrapped in a prayer shawl, mumbling into his Siddur.

We were 32 men in all, on two *Dabboor* missile boats, one of which carried the dismantled AH-IS Cobra gunship, just in case, its body wrapped in green tarp, the rotors and engine below deck. The other boat had a mini-hospital station, with 500 litres of blood supply, also in case.

Before we left, the Rabbi had tried to foist on us Bibles, as usual. To my surprise I saw it was the Yemenite Rabbi from Haifa, who had divorced me and Nitza. Probably doing reserve service. He didn't recognize me.

"We already have," I told him.

"Yes?"

"Yes, yes," I lied.

"Always," said Moosa.

The sea was calm all the way to Tunis, luckily, because I always get sea sick. But not this time. It was so calm it felt almost like a rowboat on the Yarkon river, in Tel Aviv, where Nitza and Ilan and I used to take a flat-bottomed dinghy, when we came to visit my father, and row to Seven-Mills and back.

I had taken with me a few old letters of Ilan's—he used to write to me from the time he was four, in large rounded script, telling me of butterflies, and clouds, and white cows—but I had no time to even look at them, now, on the boat. There was as usual a ton of stuff to check. The black Nomex coveralls with their thousand pockets—they tore so easily that each one of us had a sewing kit; the thick kevlar vests, which we had to oil every two hours with green olive-oil, so they wouldn't get stiff and squeak; the special night-vision goggles—these would require tuning an hour before going in; the face masks, these must fit, and I had to check everyone's; the radios, the emergency homing devices, the thousand and one weapons, Uzis, MAC-10's, Gallils, Berettas, fine-tune all those triggers, we had so much stuff it was ridiculous. I don't know, in my father's day, before the War of Independence of '48, they used to go into Cairo, or 'Aman, with nothing, just an old Arab *galabieh*, one sharp knife, and a pita and olives in their pocket, then come out after a week with the job done. I guess once you have a State everything gets more complicated, even this.

The Mossad people had tried to make us use Berettas, for the in-house job, but I insisted on silenced Uzis. I didn't care shit about deniability. Since my team was going in, it was my call, and I wanted bursts, not single bullets. So finally they caved in.

There was also one woman on board, a red-headed harridan from the Paris office of the Mossad, who came to take a video film of everything, for training later. I didn't like this part—once I threw up when I saw myself in such a movie afterwards, what I did when I was in the heat of it, but there was nothing I could do. Cabinet wanted it. I think she fucked at least three of the naval commandos, en route, maybe even Moosa. She reminded me of Nitza. They get so they don't even think it's something special.

After three days we arrived at Tunis. The coast looked just like the Herzliya beach, north of Tel Aviv—white, and with rolling sand dunes, but also with lots of palm trees, like in Azza. The water also smelled the same, with pieces of shit floating in it, and condoms. Civilization had come to the Arabs, too.

We lolled around just beyond the territorial waters for one more day, until Cabinet in Yerushalayim gave us the formal approval. They always do that, argue about "advisability," to the very last moment. I'm told this time it was really close—some leftist kibbutz ministers got cold feet, as usual. It seems there were some peace overtures afoot—maybe my father was even involved. He used to serve as a go-between in such things, even when he was minister without portfolio for shmutz, because his word was always good, for both sides. I don't know whether he pushed to have this RO cancelled or not. I never asked him. Apparently this time the peace overtures were supposed to go through the King of Morocco, the Mossad harridan said (the *shoo-shoo* people always liked to open their mouth and boast how much they knew, during operations), so an RO on his doorstep would make him look bad.

"So it will make him look bad! His mother's cunt!" Moosa shouted. "Fucking *Arabush*. Look bad! He lets them stay in Rabat also, doesn't he? Look bad, his mother's cunt!"

The Mossad woman said it was all bullshit anyway, Peace, Shmeace. "No-one will ever vote for a government that tried to talk to these fuckers. Would you vote for them? People who kill children? Like this?" she addressed first me, then Moosa, and without waiting for an answer launched into a political analysis of the next elections, and Moosa and I excused ourselves. These Mossad people, once they kill, they think they can tell the future, maybe even make it.

At last we got the green light from Yerushalayim. ("Light Unto Nations," I recall, was the code-word.)

The naval commandos went in first, looking like huge frogs bulging with malignant tumours everywhere, then piled into their ugly grey-black dinghies and rowed ashore, and after an hour clicked back their okay. So finally we went in ourselves, in two rubber dinghies, eight men in each, and I gave the sign to detach from the *Dabboor* boats. As we detached I pulled out Ilan's photo and stuck it in the breast pocket of my Nomex coverall. I knew it was a breach of security, but I don't know, he was my son, and still I had not cried over him, not even in the funeral. I don't know if this was because I had turned into a monster who felt nothing anymore, like Nitza once said, or maybe simply because the moment Yossi told me that Ilan got it, I knew I would be in on the RO, and was already under Operational Rules. But then, in one way or another I had been under Operational Rules ever since I had joined, nineteen years before, just as my father had been, ever since he had arrived in Palestine, more than 50 years ago.

It took us two-and-a-half hours to get to the shore—we couldn't use engines, not even the small electrical ones, so we let the naval commandos tug us in, swimming in the shit with their extra large flippers on. On the beach at Ras Carthage there was already a short line of cars, waiting, with Mossad people, all smoking, all trying desperately to appear nonchalant. We got in and drove down the coast, the 25 miles south to Tunis, and arrived at Abu Salam's villa at 1.40 am. Then we waited, in a side-street, lying on the floors of the cars. From time to time I took out Ilan's photo and looked at it; I don't know why: it was so dark inside the van I could see next to nothing.

Abu Salam returned an hour later, with his wife and son, in a long black Mercedes with the green-red-white Palestinian flag. His three bodyguards—two Libyans with curly hair, and a huge black American—jumped out and spread before the villa, with Kalashnikovs at the ready, like in a Charles Bronson movie, as he dashed from the Mercedes into the house, then his wife and his son. The month before, a splinter faction who had been voted off the Palestine National Council tried to take revenge on him, so I guess he was extra careful now.

For an hour after he had gone in I watched through a little mirror on a stick from across the street, in the vw van, waiting for the light to go out in his window at the second floor. Every fifteen minutes I clicked one on the radio, and Moosa clicked two back, just to let me know he was there, not asleep.

Although I tried not to, I could not stop myself from taking Ilan's picture out frequently, to look at it. In the dark his face was a mere blur, just as it was in my memory. The last I had seen him was five weeks before; lately I had been neglecting him; mostly because I couldn't stand seeing Nitza, or Yossi, how contented they seemed together, and also because I was sick of refusing her importunities every time we met. "Yossi, he doesn't mind," she said, "he told me this when we got married. In the kibbutz everybody screws on the side."

"Not me," I said to her. "I am from Tel Aviv."

"I thought they also screw in Tel Aviv, on the side."

"So maybe I don't know," I said, implying I didn't want to know.

She was not the first woman I had known; but then I didn't know that many.

You would think she would give up after a while, but no; she persisted, every time I came. So after a while I began to visit as little as possible, maybe once a month, and also because I didn't miss Ilan too much. Except in our letters, we never really got along well. He was a brooding child, wild at times, the rest of it a silent loner. On more than one occasion we sat together, drinking clotted boiled milk, in the kibbutz dining-room, looking away from each other, saying almost nothing, waiting until it was time for me to go.

It was strange, how much I missed him now, when he was gone, whereas before I could go on three, four, weeks, without thinking of him even once.

At 3:50 am the light in Abu Salam's bedroom finally went off. I waited five minutes, listening to the silence, then clicked four on the radio—Go. Moosa gave a five-click response, and the vans' doors slid open.

As Moosa's Team Bett deployed outside on the curb, nearly invisible in their light-absorbing Nomex suits, the Mossad girl strolled by and shot the Mercedes's sleeping driver with a silenced Beretta in the forehead, then she nodded to us, pleasantly, proudly, but we were already racing up the red-tile stairs of the villa—the door had been blown off its hinges with white plastic under a kevlar-styrofoam limpet—it's amazing how silent this is—and we were in. I got the two Libyan guards who were dozing at the foot of the staircase, in plush green chairs, and as we raced up the oak-wood stairs to the second floor (behind me my 2IC shot the black American, who had appeared from the basement), the door to the bedroom opened, and Abu Salam emerged, his bald head glistening with sweat, a pistol in his hand, a Tokarov. But before he could shoot, a boy jumped out of another bedroom into his arms, crying. It was his son, a thirteen-year-old blond boy. (Ilan had been a redhead, like Nitza.) The boy shouted something in French to Abu Salam, who tried to shake him off his arm, shouting to him something back, I didn't catch what it was. I know that Intelligence said the son was Arafat's catamite; but I don't know. He looked just like a boy. With freckles, even, and blue-and-white pyjamas.

Moosa's voice shouted in my earphone, "Take him down, you donkey!" I felt myself reddening with shame. I was probably a whole five seconds late. I let out a long silenced burst and got them both. Just then his wife appeared in the bedroom door, a small blonde with a pinched face, a Kalash in her hand, but my 2IC got her. As we raced back down the stairs the Intelligence team was already clattering up, with their huge suitcases, for the documents.

We threw suitcases and bags into the back of the vans, then the video girl scurried out (it came out later I had only delayed a second and a half, so it was no big deal), and we scrammed. The entire take-down took maybe 31 seconds, from the moment we blew in the door to the moment the last one left the house, a Mossad louse who had dropped his Beretta.

Three days later I rejoined the *Sayeret*, one rank below what I had had before, but who cares. Dada and the guys gave me a little party in his villa, without wives, and after we finished all the Johnny Walkers and the Stock 777s we watched the video. I didn't get sick at all, this time. It looked pretty good. Even Moosa said so. When Abu Salam fell off the banister, still clutching the boy, Dada called to me jokingly that maybe now we should start talking to them, now that we could finally understand each other, and everybody laughed almost to tears, me too.

The next day I went back to the kibbutz, to tell Nitza. (She had tried to pull strings, to come see the video, but the PM said No.) Yossi wasn't home, so after we had finished looking at old photos we fucked on the sofa. It wasn't like old times, but it was good enough. Times change, people change, you have to change if you want to live in this place. If you can bring yourself to share your woman, maybe one day you could also let yourself share your land.

Og

The Elders came for him late at night, before dawn, just like last time. Og didn't know how he knew that, but the knowledge arrived upon him even before the dank rot inside the casket turned fresher in his nostrils and the nerve-jangling creak of the sliding lid rattled his ears. As the freshness tugged at him, his consciousness floated up from the depths where it had been flung, beyond sleep, beyond death; and he felt the pain wrench his dead heart as his scarred palms grabbed the edge of casket. He heard his backbone creak as he struggled to sit up, and moist coolness stung his cheeks, perhaps morning dew, perhaps his own tears. Through the wetness, as the casket lid slid open, he saw in the grey light the clenched faces of the two Sanhedrin Elders whose names he had forgotten, but whose eyes had remained chiselled in his memory.

"How many nights have I slept?" he rasped, sitting up in his bronze-lined sarcophagus. "Two nights? Three?"

He knew it was still night because the sky beyond the crypt's marble doorway spread blue-black and dull like a dead snakeskin pockmarked with stars; and behind it, like vertical stains of ink, rose the spiralling towers of the city of Bashan. Then all at once, as the smell of dried blood and putrid wood shavings came in his nostrils—the smell of the gallows—his memories flooded back, like skittering crows plunging down to perch on a leafless oak.

"So I have been pardoned?" he whispered. More wetness stung his cheek.

The two Elders said nothing, just helped him climb out of the casket, their silken sleeves cool and slithering, their palms trembling as they touched his corded forearms.

"Take your armour and all your weapons," whispered the younger Elder. "Make haste."

Dutifully Og dug his claws under his crumpled cape, at the casket's side, where his long sword, still in its bejewelled scabbard, lay besides his steel longbow and a dozen feathered arrows—the poison-tipped ones that he himself had dipped in the green blood of desert vipers. With numb fingers he felt for his steel dirk, the throat-slasher, the hook-spiked flail, the brain batterer, and all his other equipment made illegal by Sanhedrin law. Even as his mind sought for answers, his hands were already acting of their own accord, distributing the weapons about his huge body, each item in its designated cache. "Why can't I leave my weapons here?" he asked. "The bailiffs won't let them into court." He flung the scabbard's wide belt across his chest, letting the sword hang along his back, buckled the iron clasp, then slung his long bow with one mighty twang, while the two robed Elders watched him in silence. The younger of the two, Og saw, was watching with something akin to anger. The older one watched with blank equanimity. Both smelled of camphor and balsam and perfumed water. The Temple's smell.

"Will the Sanhedrin's session last long?" Og asked. "Or has my appeal been accepted already, and this is a mere formality?" He stood up, stretched his hirsute arms, bent his knees several times and yawned. His body was stiff as if he had slept years, not just a few nights. His claws, he saw, had grown overly long, and the dark stains under the tips were now dust. . . . A violent shudder went through him as the red memory slammed into the back of his head, and the understanding. "No court session?" he croaked. "No pardon?"

"No court," the younger Elder said, spitting the words through tight white lips. "We came because—we—the Sanhedrin—we need your help—again. . . ." He breathed in spurts, his eyes narrow with distaste and hate.

Og sank down on the edge of his casket. His corded neck throbbed where the woven metal rope had tightened around it last time. And the time before that, and all the times before. Fiery red-tinged memories roared back, like an avalanche of lava. How many times did this scene happen already? How many times had they called him, and lied to him? How many times had he promised himself not to believe anymore? Has he not lost count?

"No!" he rasped. "Last time you also said you needed me! You swore it would be different! Yet once it ended, you again put me to trial for what I have done for you. . . ."

"We had said it would be different if you followed instructions! But you disobeyed," the younger Elder hissed. "You did what we expressly had asked you not to do in war—never to do—we had told you. . . ."

Og tugged his sword out of its scabbard, the blade tearing through the years of rust. Pulling a whetstone out of its cache he began to sharpen the long blade. "There was no other way. There never has been! They hide behind their women and elders as they fight; they give poisoned weapons to their children. . . ."

"No! There must have been another way."

"There was none."

"We gave you your instructions and rules of war and you ignored them—"

"There was no other way to save Bashan."

Why was he even talking back to the Sanhedrin Elders? It had always been thus. Og tested the long blade on his index claw. The sharp edge barely left a line. He went on sharpening, his eyes narrow and hot.

The older councillor spoke now, "Bashan needs you again." His voice was dispassionate, matter-of-fact, reasonable, as if speaking to a child, or a domestic animal.

Og kept on sharpening his sword. In the distance he heard a faint boom of cannon. He felt his blood freeze, then quicken.

"No," he said.

The younger Elder stuttered, "But . . . but the Midianite army has returned, and—and there's no-one else."

Og said, "Has the Sanhedrin at least heard my request for pardon, for last time's deeds?"

There was silence. The answer was clear.

"Why not?"

The senior Elder said in a coppery voice, "We told you. We could not condone such war acts. We simply could not."

"But I have done them all to save the City! They were all necessary! As always!"

The Elder shook his head obstinately. "We simply cannot condone such acts."

Og said, "But when you sent for me last time, you knew I must do something similar to the time before, to repel the Midianites. They do worse!"

"We are not them. Such barbarity, had we but known. . . ."

"But you must have known!"

Again, there was silence, cold and fluttery.

Og put the whetstone away and slid his long sword into its metal sheathe. Now it slipped in noiselessly. He said, "I will not go fight for the City this time unless I know I will be forgiven if I do again what I must, to defend it."

The two Elders looked down, then at each other, and muttered softly. The younger one spoke. "We—we are authorized to accept your condition."

"You are?"

"Yes. If you defend Bashan, nothing you do will be held against you this time."

"Nothing? Even if I have to fight their children—if I have to do what I have done before?"

The two Elders looked away. "Hopefully it will not come to that."

"And if it does? With such evil enemies, it always does."

The younger councillor's whisper was nearly inaudible. "As we said, this time you will be forgiven."

More rumbling of cannon came on the night air, and a few piercing screams.

Og stood up. "How strong is the Midianites' army now?"

"Stronger than last time. Five new brigades of children have been formed, and not only their arrows, but their teeth too are now dipped in poison. . . ."

"And ours? Bashan's army?"

"Feeble. Feebler than before."

"Why have you not re-trained? You have had how long? Three days? A week?"

"Seven years."

Og sat down in shock. "I have—slept—seven years?"

No answer.

"In seven years you could have trained Bashan's entire army to fight the Midianites and do the necessary deeds like me—"

"No, no!" The younger Elder's voice held traces of panic. "We cannot allow ourselves to teach such things! If we did, we would be no better than the barbarians!"

Og remembered he had had this conversation many times before. It was useless to argue. He rose to his feet. "Where are the Midianites camped?"

"We'll take you."

When he at last came back, covered in grime and blood and brains, they were waiting for him at Bashan's gate.

"You have won?"

"Yes." He was cut in a hundred places. His talons dripped blood. His teeth too. Gashes over his eyes were encrusted with grey-yellow muck. "I have killed them all."

"All?"

"Yes."

"How?"

He told them. "It was the only way."

"But we have told you expressly not to act this way! We have told you to adhere to the conventions of war! No atrocities, we said! Haven't we?"

Behind, he saw, a crowd of Bashan city folk was gathering, dressed in victory silks of white and blue.

"No you haven't," he said to the Elders. "You told me to do the necessary, to defend the city, and whatever I do will be forgiven."

"We certainly will not!" the younger Elder said frostily, looking him straight in the eye. "We are civilized—unlike the barbarian Midianites you have just butchered. Some things we simply won't do!"

Og knew what was coming. "At any rate, Bashan is safe. Can I go back home now, to the hills of Moab?"

"The Sanhedrin will have to decide."

Next morning was the trial.

"Seven years ago," said the Sanhedrin's speaker, the presiding judge, "you committed war atrocities. Now you have done so again, against express warnings. I judge you to be hanged, then buried inside a bronze-lined casket. May every decent Bashanite abominate your name. You are an example of what we will never let ourselves become. Take him away."

As before, they hanged him before sundown, at the city's gate, with a rope of corded steel. When he stopped twitching they wrapped his body in his velvet cape, and one by one all the Elders came by and spit on him, carefully. Then two ageing bailiffs threw the body into the casket, slid the lid into place, and secured it with chains.

"His name should be a warning to all decent Bashanites," said the judge.

They had wrapped his body well, to preserve it. Just in case.

ACKNOWLEDGMENTS

I would like to thank the following for helping make my fiction into reality:

Molly Giles and Frances Mayes of San Francisco State University's Creative Writing program, where I learned how to make words speak; Jim Frey of Berkeley, who taught me about dramatic structures; and Josephine Carson of SFSU, who taught me much about Character, both literary and otherwise; Howard Junker, editor of *Zyzzyva*, who published my first story, just like that; Neal Kozodoy, editor of *Commentary*, who published this book's title story; Nicholas Macklem and Dilshad Engineer of Oberon Press, who did such a fine job with the Canadian edition of *Talking to the Enemy*; Katrina Kenison of *Best American Short Stories*, who flabbergasted me by picking "Pity" for her 1995 anthology; Bill Henderson and the editors of the *Pushcart Prize* anthology, who picked the same story for theirs; the team at American Conservatory Theater in Berkeley, who turned "Pity" into a one-man show that caused goose-bumps; Ellen Seligman of McClelland and Stewart in Canada, who included a story of mine ("Cuckoo") in the *Journey Prize* anthology; Dan Simon and Anna Lui of Seven Stories, who did a splendid job undertaking to publish *Talking to the Enemy* in the U.S. and worldwide; and most of all, my thanks to my loyal agent, Victoria Pryor, who stuck with me throughout the years.

My sincere thanks to them all, as well as to those who edited, read, and commented on my stories. Their help was invaluable, and I couldn't have done without them.

In addition, I would like to acknowledge the ancient fiction-eers who anonymously wrote the all-time bestseller, and who, astonishingly, managed to convince half of humanity that it is entirely normal to live one's life according to antique fictions. Without this marvelously original con job, I would have little to write about.

ABOUT THE AUTHOR

Avner Mandelman was born in Israel and served in the Israeli Air Force during the Six Day War. He has a degree in aeronautical engineering from the Israeli Technion, an MBA from Stanford, and an MA in creative writing from San Francisco State University. His stories have been published in the U.S., Israel, and Canada. Avner's work has been anthologized in *Best American Short Stories*, the *Pushcart Prize*, and the *Journey Prize*. He published two collections of short stories in Canada including *Talking to the Enemy*, which won the Best Fiction Award from the Jewish Public Library of Montreal. Avner lives in Toronto with his two children, and is currently working on further short stories and a novel.

PUBLICATION IN BOOK FORM

"Pity," "Terror," "Test," "Life in Parts," and "Talking to the Enemy" were published in Canada by Oberon Press in *Talking to the Enemy*, 1998. "Black," "Mish-Mash," "Curse," and "Og" were published in Canada by Oberon Press in *Cuckoo*, 2003. "Pity" appeared in *Best American Short Stories 1995* and the *Pushcart Prize XX: Best of the Small Presses 1996*.

PUBLICATION IN JOURNALS

"Pity" was originally published in ZYZZYVA; "Test" was originally published in *The Occident* and *Ma'arv* (Israel); "Life in Parts" originally appeared in *Partisan Review* and *Ma'ariv*; "Talking to the Enemy" was first published in *Commentary*.